MAX BRAND

Author Of Millions Of Books In Print!

"Brand's Westerns are good reading and crammed with adventure!" —*Chicago Tribune*

A writer of legendary genius, Max Brand has brought to his Westerns the raw frontier action and historical authenticity that have earned him the title of the world's most celebrated Western writer.

In *Gun Gentlemen*, Lucky Bill's good fortune has just about run out. For as long as anyone can remember, the ornery dude has led a charmed life, but someone has framed him for a hanging offense. He's wanted by every tin star in the West and by every greedy gunslinger out for the price they can get for his no-good corpse. But Bill is no yellowbelly—he's aiming to clear his name and he'll take on any bushwhacker who stands in his way.

Other *Leisure Books* by Max Brand:
THE MUSTANG HERDER
WESTERN TOMMY
SPEEDY
THE WHITE WOLF
TROUBLE IN TIMBERLINE
RIDERS OF THE SILENCES
TIMBAL GULCH TRAIL
THE BELLS OF SAN FILIPO
MARBLEFACE
THE RETURN OF THE RANCHER
RONICKY DOONE'S REWARD
RONICKY DOONE'S TREASURE
RONICKY DOONE
BLACKIE AND RED
THE WHISPERING OUTLAW
THE SHADOW OF SILVER TIP
THE TRAP AT COMANCHE BEND
THE MOUNTAIN FUGITIVE

MAX BRAND

GUN GENTLEMEN

LEISURE BOOKS **NEW YORK CITY**

GUN GENTLEMEN

Chapter One

The Rivals

"Where's the sheriff?"

"He'll be on hand in time for the funeral. Hurry up; we want front seats."

Such murmurs ran behind Lucky Bill as he stepped into the Alcazar Saloon. He went with a quick-beating heart, as the actor who has many times triumphed in his favorite role feels the thrill of the first night when he steps out behind the footlights. It was the old-new thing for Lucky Bill—the curious faces of many men grown a little pale and one central figure.

He had heard of Mat Morgan, a natural battler like himself, but according to a report, one of more malice; and now he measured his man as some champion pugilist measures a challenger, hunting hungrily for the vital spot. He sought, also, for the provocation which he always needed in order to do his best. Usually men of the gun swaggered, often they were sneering, but Mat Morgan was neither the one nor the other. He stood with his back to the bar and his elbows resting lightly on it, a young fellow hardly older than Lucky Bill himself— slender, handsome in a dark way.

Just as the secondary artists draw away toward the wings when the star enters, so the men in the Alcazar scattered toward corners and back from the bar when the door opened upon Lucky Bill. The center of the stage was left for him, with only one man standing in it.

He paused a moment as the door swung behind him, ready for anything. That careless pose of the man at the bar might mean anything. It might be the means through which he hoped to pull Lucky off guard for the split part of a second; that space would be enough for the attack.

But Mat Morgan did not move. His black eyes kept steadily upon the face of Lucky, but there was neither a sneer nor a smile. Absolutely unafraid, he seemed to merely await the cue which his foe would give him. Lucky was puzzled. It was as if he were the steel and yonder fellow was the flint; they had met and yet there was no spark struck.

He sauntered on to the bar, straight to Mat Morgan.

"I hear you want to see me?" he said. "I'm Lucky Bill."

"I been controlling my impatience pretty well, but— I'm glad to see you, Lucky. I'm Mat Morgan."

He smiled a little as he spoke; not tauntingly, but rather as one who was stirred a trifle by a sense of humor. And still no spark flew. They were both at pause; Lucky, feeling that his own position was more alert than that of his opponent, hastily assumed a pose equally indifferent. He rested an elbow on the bar and found the foot rail.

"Drink?"

What else could he say to force the conversation, particularly since Mat Morgan remained so passive?

"Why, sure."

The drinks were poured, and the crowd, seeing that this was not to be a case of fire and gunpowder, blowing up at first touch. settled down to watch, as the audience settles back while the pugilists spar and feel each other out in the first rounds, yet keen-eyed and watchful lest one should stop feinting and lash out with what might be the decisive blow. So they gave plenty of room in the center of the bar to the two, and the bartender found something to busy him far away among the stacks of glasses. The antagonists were talking in low voices.

Lucky Bill, turning his glass between thumb and forefinger, had looked from his foe to his whisky alternately. He was growing embarrassed. Finally he murmured: "Suppose you tell me why you sent word you was waiting for me, Mat?"

"Sure, I will. Because you sent word first that you was hunting me, Lucky."

"I sent that word?"

"You sure did!"

"It's a lie!" said Lucky through his teeth.

The crowd caught the tone of the murmur and grew tense; the purring whispers of the two gunmen were more terrible and ominous than if they had blasphemed and shouted at each other. Mat Morgan had stiffened.

"I don't mind saying it ain't a lie," he remarked.

Lucky Bill groaned.

"A little gent with a long nose?"

"That's him."

"It's a frame, Mat. I never sent any word to you."

"Some skunk is out to get us, then. They've started us after each other, Bill. We'll just shake hands and call it square."

"But who'll leave first?"

"Why, I was in here already; it's up to you to beat it, Lucky."

But Lucky Bill frowned.

"I don't see it that way; they'd say I took water."

Still they turned their glasses and did not touch the liquor in them. Frankly, each of them liked the other, would have trusted him very far, would have chosen him even on this slight acquaintance for a friend in a pinch; but each, in deadly fear lest the other should gain an advantage in the eye of the public, watched the other with catlike steadiness. They were growing more tense now. The expectation of so many men was spurring them on, and they both knew that, sooner or later, trouble would come if they continued to face each other.

"Mat," said Lucky Bill softly, "we got to break out of this some way. If we stand here staring at each other one of us will wink pretty soon, and then there'll be a gunplay—it's in the air."

"Suppose we sit in at that poker game. They's only four of them; we'll make a full game. Getting in a crowd like that—maybe one of us will get busted and then the one that's broke can beat it."

"I'm a rotten hand at poker, but I'll take the chance. And here's to you, Mat."

All eyes drifted with them across the room. The apparent friendliness deceived no one—the two were waiting for the break in their silent, deadly little game. Mat

10

Morgan was well known in Wheeler, and as he was never noisy, his quietness now could be considered as evil as one chose. And Wheeler, to a man, chose to consider it in that light.

It was felt, in the barroom, that each was trying to break the will of the other; there had been cases like that in the history of the mountain desert. Men had fenced with each other through an entire evening, using nothing save their eyes, neither daring to withdraw or to make the first move toward a fight, until one of them would crumple suddenly and become a shivering, wild-eyed coward. Wheeler was fairly confident that such a silent duel was now about to take place, and the town quivered with enjoyment.

As for the four who had been pretending to play poker at the corner table since the entrance of Lucky Bill, they viewed the coming of the two recruits without enthusiasm. Indeed, had two lepers slipped into the vacant chairs they would have been received in the same manner. Yet when Lucky and Mat had asked permission to sit in, each of the four had hastily declared his willingness. Six chairs were now drawn up around the table, crowding each other, for the surface was small.

The others in the saloon, seeing that there was little likelihood of a sudden outbreak, now spread back toward the bar, where they gathered in groups, talking together in a murmur, as though they feared that their talk might keep them from hearing something of importance at the poker table. So that there was a continual soft background of noise in the place. It was like the sound of swarming bees heard at a distance—there was the same whining note of anger in it.

The six at the poker table now offered a study. Mat

11

Max Brand

Morgan and Lucky Bill had discreetly assumed attitudes of utmost indifference, but the other four were obviously on edge. It was one thing to sit in at a cheery game with friends. It was quite another to be present where two professional fighters were liable at any moment to whip out guns and start blazing away.

On the very first hand one of the original four began to bet recklessly. He made it twenty to come in and had hardly received his draw when, in his turn, he pushed a hundred to the center of the table. It was more than quadrupling the speed of the former game, but if he was choosing to bluff he had fallen in the wrong company. Mat Morgan instantly saw him and raised him a cool hundred.

But to the astonishment of the other, there was another raise, and so on, until each had staked a round eight hundred dollars. At that point Mat Morgan called and those at the table were staggered to see a miserable pair of nines laid down against Mat's queen full on deuces. The other pushed back his chair.

"That's what I took out of the game, boys," he said, "and I guess they ain't any objections if I quit you now."

He went away, mopping his forehead, but evidently vastly relieved.

"Cost me eight hundred," he said to a friend at the bar, "but what do I care? A whole skin is worth a pile more'n that to me; and I guess the rest of the boys must figure the same way."

As a matter of fact, on the very next hand another of the original four dropped out, though his bluff had not been quite so rank, and this time it was Lucky Bill who raked in the winnings. By this time the maneuver was plain to both him and Mat Morgan; they crossed glances in a flash of understanding.

They commenced betting on nothing, throwing good cards away, holding up nothing for the draw. But in spite of that they won. It was impossible not to, from men who were determined to lose, and after the fifth hand the last member of the original four had left the table. Mat Morgan turned in his chair and hailed a number of men by name, but no one cared to sit into that unpopular game. He turned back; in spite of all their maneuvering he and Lucky Bill were once more face-to-face.

Chapter Two

The Fight

Also, it was impossible to talk as openly as they had done at the bar. Men were standing closer now. Behind the chairs of the gamblers the space was carefully left empty, in case of a sudden drawing of guns and fusillade of bullets, but on either side men drew close, apparently to watch the fall of the cards. Mat Morgan, shuffling, cunningly flicked a card through the air so that it fell close to Lucky's chair. He leaned over, fumbled for it, and whispered:

"Lucky, what's the move? Name it, and I'm with you."

That question remained unanswered for four hands; there was not the slightest opportunity to talk. And in the meantime the strain grew. A drunkard, coming through the door, stumbled and fell prone. Not a head was turned to mark him; not an ear seemed to be able to hear anything except the monotonous murmur of the players: "See you. Raise you. Call that." Over and over again.

If the glances of the audience stirred, it was to follow the hands of the two men as they were dropped down beside them. Who knew when one of those hands would flash up, carrying a gun? The test was beginning to tell on the two. As the murmur ceased around them, and that patient waiting continued, Mat Morgan began to lose color, sitting a little stiffer and straighter in his chair.

Lucky Bill marked that, and knew the meaning. Mat was on edge, and his nerve was beginning to give way; but before that was accomplished he would fight. The explosion, Lucky shrewdly guessed, could be only a matter of minutes.

In the next deal, reaching for a random card at the side of the table, he threw his weight forward so that his chair slipped and brought his chest against the table— and the table scraped forward upon Mat Morgan.

There was an instant catching of breath in the room. Was not this the crisis at last? Had not the table been thrust forward to pin down the arms of Morgan? Mat himself seemed to guess that, for he had twisted sidewise in his chair with catlike speed and now gathered his legs under him, ready for any sort of action.

But Lucky Bill had whispered softly, under the noise of the scraping table: "Him that loses the next jackpot goes." Then he waited. The hand was dealt. Still no answer. He looked fixedly across the table and saw Morgan, staring down at his cards, nod. The jackpot, then, would decide. And he who lost must rise from that table and leave the room disgraced, beaten in the eyes of all those men.

Lucky Bill glanced over their faces, and a hot wave of blood washed into his brain. What were they but coyotes standing about waiting for two great elks to batter each other down? Then they would spring on the one that fell. And Lucky Bill hated them all, despised them all. He would not have changed the whole group for the value of Mat Morgan's little finger.

Yet to be seen to leave the barroom by these fellows, to know that they were gaping after him, that they would begin to smile the moment the door closed on him—this was maddening. No matter how long he lived, nor how many reckless deeds were marked to his credit, the story of how he lost his nerve when he faced Mat Morgan would never be forgotten.

Even should he meet Morgan later and overcome him, the affair would leave its sting, for every man who faced him thereafter would feel that perhaps this was another off day with Lucky Bill. Men who would not have dared before to take liberties with him would cross him.

Besides, the tale would grow as it spread. There would be shameful details embroidered on it as it circulated through the length and breadth of the mountain desert. Every one would believe. They were always ready to believe that some man of violence had at last fallen. But his word was pledged.

He slipped the cards back and forth across the table, bunched his own deftly together, and then flipped up the corners. Seven, nine, ten, jack, king—that was his layout. With his blood chilling, he forced his glance up, inch by inch, until it reached the face of Mat Morgan. And Mat also sat stricken with the same horror. He was forcing himself to smile, but it was a deadly effort. Their glances met; of one accord a vast relief spread through their faces. Neither of them had openers.

They sweetened the pot and dealt again. Still no openers. Again a hand, and still no pair of jacks appeared. Lucky Bill saw the fingers of Mat Morgan trembling. The man was gone; his nerve had been washed away by the crucial test, and now, under a shell of carelessness, he was a hollow spirit.

Lucky Bill knew that if he forced the fight now, it would be as easy to handle Mat Morgan as if the other were a child. But he felt no exultation as he saw this. It was merely a great pity for Mat that swept through him. Courage was of various kinds; Mat Morgan's was not of the peculiar kind needed in such a contest as this. Besides, his word had been given. The cards should decide who won this battle, and not a play of guns.

He picked up his next hand like a nervous tyro, one by one sifting the cards between his fingers. Ace, deuce, five, and—two tens! It was like knocking at the door which cannot be opened.

"Open her!" said the voice of Mat Morgan.

And looking up in his despair, Lucky Bill shoved his ante mechanically into the pot, discarded, and called for his three. Mat Morgan was holding up four! Two pairs?

He could see the triumph of Mat as plainly as though he were looking over the shoulder into his hand. The smile trembled on the lips of the other; he had lowered his eyes to control the fire that was in them. Lucky Bill closed his eyes, straightened his shoulders, and made ready. At least he would play the hand out. He picked up the three cards called for—a queen, a deuce, and ten! He stared at it in wonder. Three tens after this infinity of waiting! He set his teeth to keep from crying out, and from the corner of his eye he examined his foe. Two pairs to begin with, and now that the cards were dealt had he filled? It was impossible to guess; yet from the complacence of Mat Morgan it seemed that this must have happened. He was shuffling his hand idly, waiting.

"Bet—a dollar," said Lucky hoarsely, and he shoved his chip forward.

"See that," said Mat Morgan, and Lucky could feel his pity. "See that and raise it a dollar."

What did the money mean?

Into his mind flashed a hope that he might be able to bluff Mat, but in a moment he knew that the idea was absurd. Mat would call his hand if it took every cent he owned in the world.

"Call you," muttered Lucky Bill, and pushed in the final money of the game. He thought back to a score of other games in which he had sat at the end of a long evening when the money had been accumulated among a few players—hands where thousands changed pockets.

Mat was not hurrying in laying down his cards, not as one who relishes the discomfiture of an enemy, but rather as if he wished to disclose a brutal truth gradually. He laid down two cards—the queen of diamonds and the queen of clubs. "Openers," said Mat.

He hesitated; sweat was glistening on the forehead of Lucky Bill; vaguely he knew that all sound had ceased in the barroom, but all that he really knew and saw was that pair of queens on which all the lights seemed to have been focused. But what were the other three cards? Down came the hand of Mat Morgan. Beside the queens lay the king of diamonds and the king of hearts. Two pairs; but had he filled with the fifth card?

"And that?" asked Lucky Bill in a low voice.

The expression of Mat Morgan altered swiftly—doubt, horror coming in place of his smiling content. Hurriedly he put down the last card—the trey of spades—and Lucky Bill dumped his own hand on the table.

"Three of a kind is better, I guess?"

All at once, looking in the sick face of Morgan he felt like crying: "We'll go together; we'll stick together, Mat!" But somehow the words would not come. He leaned back in his chair, very cold, waiting and watching.

Mat Morgan, dropping his hands on the table, helped himself up with arms that wabbled, turned slowly, and walked toward the door; Lucky Bill was glad that he could not see his face. But, what was almost as bad, he could see the faces of the others as they glanced at Morgan and then stared incredulously at one another. Gradually the truth came home to them. Mat Morgan had given up without striking a blow. How were the mighty fallen in the high places of Wheeler!

And someone called: "What's the matter, Morgan? Had enough?"

Morgan whirled on his heel, his face convulsed, but he who had called was veiled by the crowd; all that Mat met was a host of mocking, scornful eyes.

"Enough of what?" he asked.

"Enough of the game, I guess?" said the bartender, and he actually winked.

Lucky Bill shuddered. Suppose he were in that situation instead of Mat Morgan. What would he do?

The bartender was speaking again. "All right, Mat. Just run along."

"Why, damn your eyes!" groaned Mat. "What d'you mean?"

But the bartender was not abashed.

"Going to take it out on me, eh?" he asked coldly. He turned to the crowd. "D'you make him out, boys? D'you begin to see the nacheral color?"

The right hand of Morgan was twitching; he was suddenly gray, as if dust had blown over his face.

"You see, Lucky," he said, turning to the other. "They ain't any other way out for me?"

Lucky Bill rose slowly.

"There don't appear to be none," he remarked calmly. "The other thing—we'll forget."

And so, in the crisis, he released Mat Morgan from his promise. There was a glint of relief and pleasure in the eye of Mat. What they had said, however, then and thereafter, was a closed book to the rest of the men in the room. One thing was clear—that the long-awaited crash was about to take place.

It was something new in the annals of barroom fights—no sudden outburst of curses; no yell of rage; no ominous whine of the fighter about to strike; but two men talking quietly, soberly. The thing seemed more deadly because it was so new.

"This is one side of the picture," declared Mat Morgan. "Maybe someday we'll turn her over and show folks the other side."

"Partner," said Lucky gravely, "I'm with you in that."

"Then—watch yourself!"

"Anytime you say, Mat."

Like two gentlemen of the old days saluting one another before the rapiers crossed!

But no rapier ever shot from its scabbard like this—so swift that nothing could be seen save a glimmer of light. Lucky Bill was watching, seeing things so clearly in the fever of his swift-moving thoughts that everything else seemed to be standing still. To the other men in the room it seemed that the hand of Mat Morgan was empty one instant, and the split part of a second later the fingers had twitched and came out bearing a flash of light at their tips.

But Lucky Bill saw the hand go back and up, saw the fingers slip around the handle of the gun.

Swift as that movement, his mind was ten thousand times faster, and he was thinking: "Mat, you're done. You're too shaky to hit the mark even if you could get your gun out fast enough. It's a rotten business, but I got to go through with it."

He even noted that the gun hung a trifle in the holster; it did not come out with the free sweep of his own weapon, that hissed against the leather and then flipped into perfect balance, snuggled against the palm of his hand. He saw the gun come out and wave a little to the right in the hand of Mat Morgan. Then, reluctantly, he pressed his own trigger.

Mat Morgan's weapon dropped unfired to the floor; he staggered back—not as one who has received a stunning blow, but rather as one who, when on tiptoe, receives a tap that knocks him off balance. The wall checked him; he stood there with his left hand pressed upon his right shoulder, and looked steadily on Lucky Bill.

But Lucky Bill had suddenly become mad; one would have said that he himself had been stung by that bullet.

21

His naked revolver was in his hand still, as he sprang to the bar and banged on it.

"You yaller-hearted, bone-spavined, splint-headed buzzards," he shouted to the crowd in the Alcazar, "get out into the street, and damned pronto! Move!"

It was, of course, extremely unreasonable, but no one cared to linger and ask the whys and wherefores. The bartender cleared his bar with a leap that brought him sprawling on the floor, and without pausing to rise to his feet he raced on all fours for the door and plowed his way through a throng of legs that were stampeding in the same direction. The door was jammed. The rear sections of the crowd swerved away from it, and dived through the windows.

In thirty seconds the sea of noise was washing far on the outside of the Alcazar, and in the barroom there was silence.

Lucky Bill had forced Mat Morgan into a chair.

"Is it bad, Mat?"

"Enough to lay me up."

"Gosh, partner, I'm sorry!"

"Sure you are. No fault of yours; just had to happen. Hey, don't start fussing around me, Billy!"

But the outer shirt of Bill was already off and had followed his vest into a corner of the room; his undershirt he was ripping into convenient strips.

"Don't talk back," he warned Mat Morgan. "But, oh, man, man, how I wish that you and me had been back to back and them coyotes against us!"

He had knotted the strips together; now he cut away the shirt of Mat Morgan.

"It's clean, boy. Never touched a bone or a tendon. You'll be as spry as ever inside two weeks! Mat, this is better to me than a hundred thousand dollars!''

But Mat was muttering: "I didn't think they was a man on earth that could of done it—got me clean before I could even get my finger on the trigger. You're a flash of light, Billy!"

"Huh! I was just lucky. That's my name, Mattie. Just plain lucky. Why, I seen what happened.'' He was busily bandaging while he spoke. "Your gun was coming like a streak when it hung in the holster. That's what got you off.''

But Mat Morgan smiled queerly at him.

"You seen my gun hang?" he asked.

"Plain as I see you."

"Well—I know you got a fast eye, partner—but I didn't think anybody living had an eye fast enough to see that! You're good, that's all I have to say."

"Who's this?" broke off Lucky Bill.

A quiet little man had stepped through the door.

"Who are you, and what d'you want?"

"Hush up, Billy. That's Jud Nevil, the sheriff.''

"How are you, sheriff?"

"Oh, fair enough. I guess you're Lucky Bill?"

He looked quizzically from one gunman to the other.

"Some call me that, but I'm off my luck tonight."

"You'll be coming along with me, Bill.''

"How come?"

"Assault with intent to kill."

"Listen to me, sheriff," said Mat Morgan. "You're wrong. They was just a little accident."

The sheriff shifted his quid so that a knot stuck out in the center of his cheek. He stepped close and lowered his voice.

"If you don't lay no charge, Mat, they ain't any arrest. Now, Bill, I dunno what your game is here, but I got this to say: Leave me alone, and I do the same for you. Good night.''

"That's what I call sense in a man," murmured Bill, turning back to his companion. "Thanks for giving me a word, Mat."

"That's nothing."

"You look pretty glum, Mat."

"Lucky, I'll tell you why. I'd rather you'd shot me through the head ten days ago than through the shoulder tonight."

"Because of the crowd that was around, partner? Don't think about 'em twice. If ever I hear any of 'em talk about this, I'll shove what he says back through his teeth."

"Damn the crowd. I can take care of that gang. Take the ten best men in the world and put 'em all together, and you have a mixup that's part coward, part sneak, and mostly fool. I ain't afraid of no crowd, Lucky, or what they say much. But you've stopped me in the middle of a journey, Bill. That's what eats into me. But— they's no use talking about it."

"Only two weeks, partner."

"Two weeks—two years—two centuries. All same thing. If you miss a mark by an inch or a promise to your girl by a minute, it's all the same thing—you're done."

"A girl?" said Lucky Bill, and he whistled.

"You ain't much for 'em?"

"Got me wrong, Mat. I like 'em all—tall and short, fat and lean, young and old; I never met anything in skirts between fifteen and sixty that wasn't old enough to teach me something and yet young enough to give

24

me a good time. You can learn how to ride a hoss and how to handle one gun as good as the next; but every time I meet a girl I feel like it was the first day of school.''

"Pardner, your ideas and mine are uncommon like each other—except that they's only one of 'em for me.''

"And it's her I've cut in on?''

"We won't talk about it.'' Mat writhed in the chair.

"That hole in your shoulder acting up, old man?''

"No, but the thought of the skunk that's going to beat me out with her is tearing me all up.''

"Listen, Mat. We got a tolerable large room all to ourselves. Talk it out.''

"Can't. If I could write a book it wouldn't be big enough to hold her.''

"But you was going down country to meet her?''

"To marry her.''

Lucky Bill groaned.

"When I don't show up, like as not she'll take the other gent just to show she can get along without me. Of course her folks like me the way a bull likes red, and this Harry Landrie, with his coin and his family and all that has been getting all their encores. But Landrie is Molly Aiken's idea of a bad time; her folks kept putting him in her way till finally she up and writes to me: 'Come down and take me; I'm tired.' Just like that. That's Molly's way.

"If I come down now and run away with her, she'll be the best wife that ever a man had. If I'm a day late she may marry Landrie or run away with the next gent. She wants action—she'll get it. That's Molly!''

"Write her a letter.''

"It'd be stopped in the mail. Her folks know my hand."

"Suppose I took that letter?"

"Lucky, it's a long ride!"

"I'll be there. Write the letter."

"No; she'd hate a letter on principle. She asks for me; I send her a letter. A kid asks for candy, and you give him beefsteak. What does he do? Throw it on the floor. That's Molly's way!"

"Mat, d'you know what's going to happen? I'm going down and take that girl away from home and bring her up to you. You just have the minister roped and ready to brand."

"You're wild, Bill."

"I ain't. I'm full of sense. Mat, I know I'm right. I'm superstitious, and I got a tingle in the tips of my fingers that tells me I'm right."

"She wouldn't come with you."

"Then I'd take her by force."

"Couldn't be done."

"I've handled a thousand-pound mustang, son."

"You've got lots of talents, Billy. But listen. She wrote: *Meet me beside the three big cottonwoods at eleven thirty.* That's tonight. Well, Billy, if I'm one minute late, or go to the wrong place, I've lost her. That's the way she is. And if the wrong man comes I'm done. She doesn't ask for reasons; she just sees facts."

Lucky Bill rubbed his brown knuckles against his chin.

"What sort of a looking girl?"

"Well, when you see her you'll know she's Molly Aiken, and you'll know why I'm in such a rush to get to her."

"From what you've told me, she's some girl, partner. Suppose—"

"Oh, I'll trust you, Billy. Would you sure make the ride? Then get her and bring her up the country. I'm going to get a buckboard and go home, and home is a shack eight miles out on the west road—red roof—anybody'll tell you where Mat Morgan lives."

"Then go out there and wait for me. I'll come and I'll bring her with me. Good-bye, Mat!"

The final instructions for finding the Aiken ranch were given, and he held out his hand, but Mat Morgan looked up at him with a mirthless smile.

"Can't raise my right hand, Billy. And I don't shake with the left. So long, boy, and—thanks!"

The big man waved gayly, and a moment later the swinging doors had closed behind him. The silence which he carried with him extended over the street, but a moment later the murmur rose and swept toward the Alcazar Saloon. First to reach it was the padding of bare feet.

Mat Morgan, rising from his chair, found a ragged little urchin beside him. Upon his head sat a sombrero so huge that it had to be tilted far back to keep it from covering his eyes, and the brim, ragged and limp from countless years of hard usage, sagged about the berry-brown face.

He wore a vest without a coat, cowpuncher fashion— it hung loosely about the agile body. A pair of man's trousers were cut off at his knees to give freer play to the bare legs and feet below—the edges of cloth had frayed, and loose edges were hanging. Yet it was not a cumbersome costume—rather it gave an impression of comfortable looseness fit for a free spirit. And such was this child. His face was as thin as the face of a man drawn by labor; but the nose and the brilliant gray eyes were the features of childhood.

Balanced deftly upon one leg, he rubbed the calf thoughtfully with the leathery calluses of the opposite foot and surveyed Mat Morgan with neither fear nor horror.

"Looks to me, Mat," he said, "like you'd been having a bad time."

The man flushed.

"We all got to have our accidents," he declared. "My gun hung in the holster."

There was no answer; but although the wide, straight mouth of the boy remained perfectly sober, there was a telltale wrinkling about his eyes. They became bright pools of mirth.

"Besides," argued Mat Morgan, "my trigger hung on me."

The youngster spoke at last.

"One good lie," he said deliberately, "is better'n half-a-dozen little ones. But that there yarn is the grand-dad of 'em all, I guess."

Mat Morgan, forgetful of himself, clenched his fist, and then remembered.

"Do me a good turn for a dime, Bud?"

"I'll do you the favor without the dime. Speak up, Mat."

"Can you get Harry Landrie for me?"

"Sure."

"Bring him to the Empire. Hurry."

For now other footsteps approached, and the curious, noisy crowd rolled back into the saloon.

Chapter Three

Man's Pay

The face of Harry Landrie was as long and canny as his body was short and broad. That face was pale with anxiety, and his long, powerful arms dangled awkwardly at his side when he stepped into Mat Morgan's room at the Empire Hotel. Bud preceded him, and now stood inside the door with his hat cocked wisely over one eye, looking from the face of one man to the other with an impish grin.

"Here you are, Mat," he said.

"And here's your dime, Bud."

The latter caught the coin as it flashed past him and juggled it in the palm of his hand.

"Mat," he said, "I done a dollar's worth of persuading to get Harry here."

"You ain't a hired man," growled Morgan. "That'll buy you candy."

"Say, Mat, when a boy does a man's work he'd ought to get a man's pay. So long."

He snapped the coin into the air. It glittered in a long arc and fell accurately into the lap of Mat Morgan; when the latter looked up Bud had disappeared through the door.

This left the two men confronting one another, and Harry Landrie became more and more ill at ease.

"That kid," he said, by way of opening conversation,"is going to come to a bad end."

"He knows too much," nodded Mat. "See if he's outside the door, will you?"

Landrie glanced hastily out into the hall; then he turned again, to the other man.

"You're kind of curious why I want to see you, Harry?"

"I dunno. Yes, I guess I am."

"Seeing that you and me ain't been pals, you'll wonder a pile more when I tell you that I'm asking a favor of you. Partners, Harry; that's what I'm asking you to play with me tonight; afterward, we play lone hands again, but tonight we can team it."

The other nodded; but his dubious glance fell on the wounded shoulder of his companion and rested there.

"I ain't an active partner," grinned Mat Morgan. "You'll do the work."

There was a silence, each studying the other.

"Harry," said Mat suddenly, "what d'you think is on top in my mind?"

"Molly Aiken," said the other after a touch of hesitation.

"Wrong. She was on top till a few minutes ago. Then a gent met me, and, through a piece of bull luck, plugged me. Lucky Bill is on top in my mind, Harry."

Again the silence. The bright little eyes of Harry Landrie bored into the dark face of Morgan.

"I'm going to get him," went on Mat. "Sooner or later he's my meat. But seeing I'm laid up now, it's apt to be a lot later. That's where you come in."

"I'm to bump off Lucky? Thanks!"

"No. You're only to get him bumped off."

Harry Landrie smiled, a slow-spreading grimace.

"I ain't a gunfighter, Morgan, and you know it. You figure to run me in on Lucky Bill. You get me killed, which leaves you clear with Molly Aiken. You get Lucky Bill outlawed for killing me, and that puts you even with him. It ain't a bad idea, partner, but I still got eyes to see things with."

"Trouble is, you see too much. Outlawing Bill wouldn't put me even. You can't feed a man hay and a hoss meat. Bill got my blood, and they ain't more'n one way he can pay me back. Now, we talk turkey."

Harry Landrie shook his head.

"We don't. We ain't friends, Morgan. You're out to get Molly Aiken. I'm out to get her, too. That makes it bad medicine to mix up in any deal together. So long, Mat."

"Wait!"

Landrie whirled.

"I got to talk unpleasant stuff, Harry, if you take it that way. I can make you talk turkey, Harry, and here's where I do it."

"This sounds more natural—seeing it's between you and me. How you going to *make* me?"

"It's a little story. Let's go back. Tonight you hear that I'm coming into Wheeler, eh?"

"Maybe. Why?"

"We'll, suppose you sit down and say to yourself: 'Mat Morgan is coming into Wheeler. Why? Wheeler ain't one of his hangouts.' "

"They's no reason why I should start figuring where you go and why."

"Wait a minute. I'm just supposing, maybe. Let me get through. You say to yourself: 'Maybe Mat Morgan knows I been bothering Molly a good deal lately. Maybe he knows that I've made a dicker with Molly's dad.' "

Harry Landrie started.

" 'So he's coming into Wheeler to get me. He's come in to murder me. That's why he's here.' Now, you send down a little long-nosed skunk named Conover to hang out in the Alcazar Saloon, knowing that I'll go there when I first hit town. Conover gets orders to report the minute Mat Morgan shows up. But while Conover is there he hears that Lucky Bill has come to town. Soon as Mat Morgan comes in, Conover goes back to you and tells you that I'm around. Also, he tells you Lucky Bill is here.

"First you think of saddling that red roan of yours and beating it. Then you get another idea. Why not play Bill against Mat Morgan? You send Conover down. He comes to me and says: 'Morgan, Lucky Bill is in town and says he's looking for you.' Then he goes over and says to Lucky Bill: 'Lucky, Mat Morgan is waiting for you in the Alcazar.'

"You knew I couldn't dodge Lucky in public. You knew Lucky couldn't dodge me after he'd been challenged like that."

Harry Landrie began backing slowly toward the door; he was arrested by the voice of Mat Morgan, lowered, but ringing: "And you planned to get me bumped off with Lucky Bill! Eh?"

"You're raving, Mat."

Morgan took one of those long chances which, occasionally, pay heavily.

"Don't lie. Conover told me."

The blow went home. Harry Landrie winced.

"The rat!" he cried. "The dirty rat!"

Mat Morgan laughed.

"He didn't tell me, but I thought a guess wouldn't do no harm. I guess he works for his pay hard enough. Well, Landrie, suppose I was to get the sheriff and tell him that little story about how you cooked up the deal?"

"Nobody in Wheeler would believe it."

"They ain't all your friends in this town."

"To hell with 'em!"

"Sure. But on a jury they're more apt to see you that way. Besides, Conover couldn't stand the gaff as a witness. I'd have a lawyer that would turn him inside out, and after what he said, you'd be done around here, Landrie. All done. Now do you listen?"

Landrie slumped heavily into a chair.

"Start going," he said, and scowled at his companion. "But don't figure on me matching Lucky Bill in a gunfight. I'm not that kind of a fool."

"I know what you are." The wrath which he had been controlling turned Morgan pale for an instant. He regained his self-possession at once. "First, I let you in on a secret. Molly and me planned to run off together tonight."

This item drew Landrie forward in his chair, as Mat noted with intense interest.

"You're a queer one, Landrie. Nothing but the name of that girl will make you fight."

"Stop your damned chatter and talk straight. What about you and Molly Aiken?"

"First place, she don't like you, Harry. Not that I figure saying it will stop you. You're the kind that wants a girl any way you can get her. Fair or foul is all the same. Well, let it go."

"To hell with your morals. You say Molly is going to break away with you tonight?"

"She was, Harry, but my friend Lucky Bill put a burr under my saddle, and the party is called off. But the point is, Molly will be waiting beside the three big cottonwoods at eleven-thirty tonight. I thought it would be a shame to spoil her party altogether. So I sent down Lucky Bill to get her for me."

"Lucky Bill!"

"You think I'm fool enough to figure that he'd take her to me the way he promised? Nope. He'll get her and keep her if he can. I could see it in his eye. But Lucky Bill is loping straight for the Aiken ranch now."

Landrie groaned and sprang to his feet. "How long ago did he start?"

"Half an hour."

"Too late, then! Morgan, you devil! You throw her away because you couldn't get her yourself! You throw her away to keep her from me!"

He was walking slowly toward Mat while he spoke. All sense of fear had gone from his face; and even Mat Morgan was impressed and watched him come with slightly widened eyes.

"Steady!" he warned. "Keep hold on yourself. You think I'm telling you all this to bother you, Landrie? No, but I'm telling you because I'm going to show you how you can beat out Lucky Bill, save Molly from being carried off, and make a hero out of yourself without ever risking your hide in gun range. Point is, I told Lucky the way to the ranch, but I told him the long way. You take your red roan the short way, and you'll save an hour. That'll give you time to warn old Aiken.

"You and him and some of his boys can cache yourselves away near the cottonwoods, and when Lucky comes and tries to persuade Molly to clear out with him—and you can lay to it that she'll fight before she'll trust herself to a stranger—the lot of you blaze away, and there's the end of Lucky Bill. Is that simple?"

The simplicity of it glazed the eyes of Harry Landrie, and then a gradual glimmer rose in them.

"Where do you come out of all this?"

"I have Lucky Bill where I want him."

"And what does it mean to me?"

"Why, you fool, won't old Aiken be grateful to you for saving the girl to him?"

"You'd risk letting me do all that?"

"I'll bet myself against you in spite of that, to get the girl in the end. But I'd risk ten like Molly Aiken to get back at Lucky Bill. My gun hung—but who'd believe that? They think he beat me to the draw. They think I've been beat once, and now every hobo on the ranges will be willing to take a chance with me—figuring he may be as lucky as Bill was. That's why I'm going to get him! Now go climb on your hoss, Harry, and raise dust."

Chapter Four

The Abduction

Lucky Bill rode with the blitheness of a man about to do a good deed. His mustang, kept cunningly just within his strength, had covered the distance to the ranch with a lope wolflike and tireless, and so the big rider saw, as Mat Morgan had pictured them, the buildings of the Aiken ranch tumbled across a hollow—a big establishment, and to the right, under the head of a hill crowned by three tall cottonwoods, a solitary horse.

Coming closer, he made out the saddle on the animal, and a figure beside the horse which now mounted and rode a few paces to meet him. Lucky Bill brought his mount to a dogtrot, and then halted in easy eye range. The moon was low, but very bright through the thin mountain air; the hill crests were etched jagged and clear against the sky; every bush was visible on the most distant of those slopes; and Lucky saw Molly Aiken clearly.

The shadow of the wide-brimmed sombrero, to be sure, fell like a mask across the upper part of her face, but he could see the nose, the mouth, the chin in a white light. He remained motionless, speechless for a moment, taking in the details of the picture and guessing at the unseen.

"You're Molly Aiken?" he asked, raising his hat and lowering it again slowly.

"Most likely," said the girl. "Here's the Aiken ranch behind me."

"Sure, but I'm not guessing at you. Mat told me you'd be here."

He welcomed the little start of her surprise.

"And your name?" she asked.

"Mostly called plain Bill. Some call me Lucky Bill."

He added this title with some hesitancy, and he was not surprised when she gathered her reins taut and swayed somewhat forward in the saddle, as one preparing for a sudden movement. After all, Bill would have been just a bit disappointed if his name had not roused a little alarm.

"I see you know me?"

"I've heard of you," replied Molly Aiken dryly.

"I'm to take you to Mat," went on Lucky smoothly. "He couldn't come; so he sent me instead."

At this she moved her horse and came close enough to study his face. She seemed rather bewildered than afraid.

"I don't know what you're talking about."

"They's time to explain," said Lucky. "We don't have to hit the trail for five minutes. They's that long before eleven thirty."

"Mat Morgan sent you?"

"Yes."

"You're a friend of his?"

"Yes."

"I never heard him speak of you."

"We ain't known each other for long."

"How long?"

"Since tonight."

She drew her horse back again.

"And he sent you to me?"

"He did."

"For what reason?"

"To take you to him."

"He couldn't come?"

"He's been shot."

"Ah!"

"Not bad; just enough to lay him up."

She waited.

"Where?"

"Through the shoulder. Nothing bad. No bones touched and no sinews cut; just through the flesh. He'll be as good as ever in ten days, I guess."

"He gave you a letter?"

"He said a letter wouldn't make no difference to you."

"Mat said that?"

"He said you'd make up your mind about me all by yourself."

At this she smiled a little.

"That sounds like Mat. But—who shot him?"

"I did."

"You—and then he sent you?"

"Sounds queer, don't it?"

"It does."

"The point is, it's too queer not to be straight stuff that I'm telling you."

"Where are you to take me?"

"Eight miles out of Wheeler on the West road, to Mat's place."

"That's where the shack is," she brooded. She raised her head and stared steadily at him again.

"I'm not going, Lucky Bill. I don't think I can."

It was so abrupt and unexpected a refusal that Lucky waited a moment, gathering strength for the crisis. He steadied his mind and his nerves with far more care than he would have done had he been facing a formidable man.

Had he been a little wiser in the ways of women he would have known that that last qualifying phrase was an unqualified submission. If he had allowed her to take matters into her own hands she would have been trotting her horse beside him; and all that was to follow would have been far different. Instead, he drew out his watch and looked at it.

"It's eleven thirty," he explained, dropping the watch back into his pocket, "and the time for talk is over. We got to have some action now."

He pushed his horse closer to her.

"Do you mean you'd force me to go with you?"

"That's a short way of saying what I'd use a pile more words for."

"I won't go a step, Lucky Bill."

"Think it over quick. Mat expects us to be on the road by this time. I got no time to be polite."

He saw a small hand flash back to the revolver which hung at the side of her saddle.

"Not a step!" she repeated.

At this Bill checked his horse, but he grinned at her.

"Let's get each other straight," he said. "You know I ain't intending to do you any harm. You know every word that I've said to you is true. What's keeping you from going with me and trusting me just as much as you'd of trusted Mat here is that you just feel stubborn. That's all they is to it. Well, lady, I'm sort of stubborn myself. I was made with an extra share of mule mixed up in me. So you're coming with me."

Had his diagnosis been less exact she would perhaps have yielded, or had there been a shade of appeal instead of a covert threat she would have submitted instantly. As it was, she suddenly hated this big, confident fellow.

"I warn you," said the girl through her teeth, "that I won't go with you."

The gun came out a little from its holster as she gathered the butt in her fingers.

"Lady," said Lucky Bill, grown very grave, "I see you still got the wrong idea about me. I know you got lots of nerve and plenty of head; but you ain't going to bluff me. In the stories the ladies sometimes shoot a man. Out in real life it ain't done unless it's a greaser or a drunken husband that gets the lead. I ain't a greaser, and I ain't your husband, and I ain't drunk. And you ain't going to shoot that gun. So don't be foolish and take it out of the holster. Put it up, and talk sense."

He swung his horse still more; his hand fell on the bridle rein.

As for Molly Aiken, she abandoned her gun as he had foreseen she would. The entire trouble was that he had foreseen too much. Somehow, she felt that he was bullying her. He had stepped into her mind, which is the

40

last offense that a man can offer to a woman. Feeling that she was lost, she was instantly determined to resist to the death. Also, she was curious; just as a child is curious about pain and pricks himself with a pin to see how much he can endure.

"Do you actually mean you would force me to go?"

"I've said I would. Are you coming?"

"Not a step!"

He swung his mustang beside hers, caught the reins from her hands, and with a dexterous touch of his spurs, set both horses in forward motion. And then the girl suddenly threw up her head and screamed.

He knew the moment her sombrero brim flared up what she was going to do, and his gloved hand flew up to stop her mouth; but as the moon fell fully upon her face, and he saw the flash of her eyes for the first time, his raised hand hesitated. In that instant the cry cut past him and rang across the hills. A moment later the glove had stopped her mouth.

Suddenly she began to fight furiously, blindly, striking with both hands, twisting to throw herself from the saddle; but with one arm around her he crushed her into the saddle, and his other hand covered her mouth. She began to choke.

"You see it ain't any use," he explained. "I ain't going to let you go. This here dirty old glove is going to stay fast over your mouth till you raise your right hand. That'll be a sign that whatever else you do you won't make no more noise. Otherwise, you just sit here and keep on choking till you're through."

Over the rim of his glove, her eyes turned and blazed at him; and then her right hand went up slowly.

"Good!" Lucky Bill sighed and dropped his hand at once.

"I'm sorry, Miss Aiken."

"Don't speak to me. Don't!"

He sighed again, and fell back a little from beside her. But as the horse went back, she looked askance. The moonlight struck well across his face, and very bright. She saw that his skin was beaded with perspiration, and his mouth set grimly as though he had been through a fierce battle.

It rallied her spirits in a queer manner. Just an instant before she had been too much afraid to be truly angry; but the moment she saw that he was not a bully capable of treating a woman like a man; the moment she discovered that he was in an agony of chivalrous shame because he had had to treat her roughly; the moment she was sure that, in the last analysis she could trust him utterly, that moment her fear left her and hot rage boiled up through her veins.

It was the anger of a child thwarted by a nurse. She rode with his fist doubled over the reins. She was in the same mood which makes a child sit down on the pavement in public and refuse to budge. She glared at Lucky Bill.

For the instant wild tales of the past of this man flooded through her mind and made her tremble again— Lucky Bill, the reckless gambler, the lover of chance, the glorious in battle, the slayer of men. It occurred to her that she was probably the only living person in the mountain desert who had ever drawn a gun to Lucky Bill and remained in existence to tell about it. The fear returned, but only for a second.

Then she saw the cleanly-cut, rather boyish profile of

Lucky, the finely poised head, with the chin carried high, the mighty breadth of those solid shoulders, prophetic of illimitable power. A man so big, she felt, could not be vicious. This thing is true, that a fearless man inspires other men with fear, but he makes women brave; the man before whom a woman trembles is the cowering sneak whom other men crush under heel.

He rode with his head turned a little toward her, though his eyes kept straight before them on the trail. There was a singular deference in his attitude, as one who said mutely: "I have gone too far; I regret it; I would do much to make amends."

She noted this with sullen fierceness. She wanted to have Lucky Bill overwhelmed with enemies; see him almost shamed; in danger; and then save him—throw his freedom scornfully at his feet. She guessed that that would be the way to bend his free spirit.

She was so busy thinking about herself and Bill that she forgot her singular situation, riding with a man whom she had never met before through the mountain desert.

Then a door slammed far behind them and wakened a tiny echo—it was like the crack of a rifle among the hills. Voices were calling, weird with distance. Yes, they had heard her cry. First they would run to her room, find that she was gone; some one, trembling, would carry the news to her father.

She could see him rise slowly, crushing the newspaper in his hand, and daring them with his eyes to repeat the tidings. He was a stern man, this father of hers. All her life she had hated him heartily, and loved him with the whole of her passionate nature. The reason was that she was very much like him. He had the strength of a man

43

and the sullen fierceness of a spoiled child—just as she had. She saw herself in him and feared him; he saw himself in her and feared her.

He would have sold his ranch for a song and sold himself into slavery to gain the means of gratifying the least of her many whims; but he would have starved her in her room with the cruelty of an Indian if she went counter to the least of his commands. And Molly Aiken would have burned at the stake to please him; and she would have seen him burned rather than submit to his pride.

They had had terrible scenes many times—scenes in which their voices were never raised, and in which their eyes threatened each other with dire calamities. After a quarrel they were always ready instantly to fall into each other's arms; but each would have suffered deadly pangs rather than make the first step toward a reconciliation.

She was building the picture, now, of her father rushing out of the house. He would shout to the bunk house; the men would pour out; there would be a flurry of saddling and mounting. She smiled grimly, looking as clearly into her father's mind as through a window on a room. He would be half eager to save her from impending danger, half furious that she had started to flee.

Instantly she wanted to foil him. Had he not the very week before threatened her solemnly if she ever dared to so much as send a message to Mat Morgan? Had not that been the sole reason that she wrote the impulsive note to the gunfighter? Indeed, she had been half relieved that it was not Mat himself who came for her.

"The spur!" commanded Lucky Bill. "They're coming!"

"Do you think I'm going to help you escape?" cried

the girl, drawing back on her reins.

He leaned close to her; his face was pinched with shame, but his eyes were frowning and resolute. In fact, her heart went out to him with sympathy, but she schooled her face to a cold contempt.

"Listen to me, lady. I put through what I start. You ride hard, and ride with me, or else I use the spur on your horse.

"If you try to yell and warn them where we are, I'm going to gag you with this bandanna. That's straight. Are you with me?"

"I hate you!" moaned Molly Aiken.

"Sure you do. That ain't the question. Will you start?"

There was no doubt that he was in earnest; furious, she touched her horse with the spurs and they went forward at a run. Over the next sweep of hills—at the very crest, he called, "Halt!" and they brought their horses to a plunging stop.

Around the shoulder of the hill to their right streamed a cavalcade of some dozen men, black in the moonlight—with their black shadows rushing beneath them. They poured through the narrow little valley with the moonshine gleaming and winking on naked guns. First of all rode a man on a big, smooth-running bay—the wind of the gallop had blown the brim of his hat straight up, and the girl recognized, with a thrill of love, pride, and hate, her father.

"Not a sound," whispered Lucky Bill beside her.

How could he tell that she would rather have had her tongue torn out than utter a syllable that would bring her father upon them? What she wanted was to return of her own free will. To be forced back would be an

45

agony greater even than death.

But the procession crashed through the valley, dipped with a yell over the next rise of ground, and was instantly cut away to a murmur.

She was aware of Lucky Bill saying: "You've played square. You *are* square. One yell would have meant the finish for me."

"You could have gotten away before they reached you."

He did not seem to understand.

"Run away from them?" he muttered, wondering.

It let in a light upon him; she understood for the first time how much iron was behind that boyish smile. The bloody tales about Lucky Bill, which the moment before had seemed ridiculous exaggerations, were suddenly made less than the truth. A man who would die to perform a promise to another man!

He had sent his horse into a steady lope, and she followed. Vaguely she felt that this was all wrong—that she must be turning back to the ranch house. But also, she felt that it had been pleasant to hear that word of praise from Lucky. And besides, a current of rising excitement was taking her up and sweeping her along. The thread which had tied her to the commonplace all her life had been snapped. She was adrift in a wind of adventure, carried without her volition.

Of course Lucky could not pry into her mind and understand all this. But he felt that she was submitting as one in a dream; any moment the dream might leave and she would resist fiercely. And Lucky was beginning to know that if it came to a crisis he would not have the courage to touch her again.

He, also, was beginning to want to turn back. For

thinking of this girl as the wife of Mat Morgan, he felt that there was something very wrong. He was not a thoughtful man. Brain problems always confused Lucky; but now he was acutely conscious of a pain.

As he looked at the girl the breath left him just as if he had been drenched to the breast in cold water. Not that she was lovely. But the white moon on her mouth and on the proud, beautiful chin, seemed symbolical to Lucky. It showed him the purity of the soul in Molly Aiken. Every now and then as they swung down the slope he recurred to the thought that once given to Mat Morgan she was given for all time.

It was mysterious. Give a horse to a man and it would come back to you, perhaps, unharmed, the same. But once a woman were given to a man, he took from her that which no other human being would ever find in her again.

He found himself saying to himself: "If I'd hurried my shot a little—if I'd fired a bit lower and to the center, Mat Morgan would be deader'n hell."

The thought did not displease him. But if Mat had died, he—Lucky—would not be riding at the side of the girl at this moment.

Mysterious are the ways of Providence, thought Lucky. But he thought it in untranslatable slang, mixed with curious curses.

In the bottom of the valley they found a well-worn cattle path, and with a gesture he invited the girl to lead the way, riding first along it. The path cut due north, the direction in which he now wished to travel.

She turned in her saddle and looked back at him.

"Suppose I let out my horse; I think he'd beat yours."

"Let me assure you he wouldn't beat my gun, though."

For a moment she still sat in the saddle, wavering with the walk of her mount, and turned straight toward Lucky. Then she swung about and sent her pony into a soft dogtrot.

As far as he could tell, her expression had been rather thoughtful than horrified when he had so calmly threatened to shoot her horse if she attempted to flee. No doubt she was deciding that he was par excellence a brute.

"Ain't it hell?" muttered Lucky to himself. "Every move I make I show myself a skunk to this girl!"

His meditations were abruptly cut into by a little cry from the girl. He looked up. They were rounding the shoulder of a hill on the cattle path, and straight down upon them, as they dipped into the hollow beyond, came a rider trotting a horse that limped terribly with the off foreleg. It was Harry Landrie!

Chapter Five

Man to Man

A few yards off the hurrying horseman saw them,
checked his mount.

"Molly!" he cried.

"Harry!" she called in turn. "Thank heaven you've
come!"

"Off to the right!" commanded Lucky Bill.

She obeyed him with singular complacence and sat on
her horse to the side, looking from one man to the other.

"Back home, Molly!" cried Harry Landrie. "Give
him the spur. They ain't any time!"

"Wait a minute!" cut in Lucky. "I'm just getting the
drift of this. You're Harry Landrie, partner?"

"That's my name. Bill, the game is up!"

"Is it? No, it's just begun, son. This girl is going
through on this way."

But Harry turned again to the girl, instead of answering.

"Molly, he came with a fake message from Mat Morgan. Ain't that right?"

The girl jerked up her head and stared at Lucky.

"Well, that message is a lie. Mat ain't sent for you. He told me—"

"You talk a pile too much," said Lucky. "If you got an argument, they's another way of putting it. What's to keep you from taking her back home? Nothing but me. You first, Landrie. Now go for your gun!"

A wind through the hills had lifted his sombrero's brim as he spoke, and the girl saw his face, pale by that light, with the bandanna fluttering at his throat. She did not wait for Landrie to reply, and she did not see the burly fellow wince at the mention of a gun play.

"No, no!" she called to them. "Harry, don't touch your gun. It'd be murder! Lucky Bill, if you're a man you won't fight that way!"

The blood ran again in the chilled heart of Landrie.

"On foot or on hoss, with guns or knives of fists," said Lucky, "I'm with you any way say, Landrie, and we'll fight it out. She's going through with me."

Now, it is an old truth that men afraid in one emergency are brave in others. Some burly athlete will shrink from gunfire where a pallid clerk shows himself a hero. The thought of a gunfight turned the blood of Harry Landrie to water; but he was a boxer with both cunning and courage.

He had been taught by professionals to use those burly fists and all the strength of the corded muscles in his long shoulders. He knew how to plant the weight of his great shoulders behind his punches; he knew the fence of footwork that sweeps a man into range and out again. And at the challenge from Lucky his eyes glowed. It was an unexpected joy to Harry to be able to show his courage and his nerve before the girl.

"Fists?" he repeated anxiously. "Did you say fists, Lucky?"

"I say it over again."

Harry swung himself from the saddle and stretched out his arms.

"I'm waiting. There's my gun on the ground. There's my knife beside it. Come on, Lucky Bill!"

"And give the girl a chance to run?" growled Lucky.

Harry threw himself eagerly on this opening. The last thing he wanted was to have Molly Aiken absent during the one instance he would ever have, perhaps, to show her his bravery and strength. For in a country where men wore guns, what did his strength and cleverness signify?

"She'll stay where she is," he asserted. "Molly, will you do that for me? Stay right where you are. No, get off your hoss and take charge of the guns."

She answered better than with words by dismounting.

"I'll keep the guns."

"And when this is over," said Lucky dubiously, "you'll give back the guns—you'll play square—you'll go on with me if I clean him up?"

"You don't seem anxious to fight," said the girl coldly. "Maybe fists aren't much in your line, Lucky? Bullying women comes easier to you!"

Lucky Bill threw the reins over the head of his horse and sprang down; he handed his gunbelt to the girl.

"You've promised?" he said.

"On my honor."

"Good," answered Lucky curtly. His knife he tossed

at her feet, and then went to meet Harry Landrie; the latter circled and came between him and the girl. The moment he had obtained this position his manner changed.

"Hark at me, Lucky," he said fiercely. "Here's where you leave your luck behind you. I know you. Murder is your line, but now that I've got you man to man, d'you know what I'm going to do? I'm going to bust you, Bill. I'm going to beat you to a pulp. I'm going to make you get down on your knees and beg. That's what I'm going to do.

"When I'm through I'm going to take your gun and your belt for a souvenir and show them to the boys. I'm going to mark you so's you'll never forget it. You been working all your life with guns, ain't you? You're sure death with 'em, ain't you?

"Well, fists is the same for me. I've worked with them same as you with guns. I've boxed an hour every day. I'm just saying it to let you know what's coming. You got no more chance agin' me than you have of dropping over a thousand-foot cliff and coming off alive!"

He lowered his voice to a snarl toward the end of this speech, and began stalking his foe in the approved pugilistic method, his left foot advanced, feeling the way deftly, his weight thrown back on his crouched right leg. His great left arm extended—his right fist drawn back before the shoulder from which place it could drive out with bone-breaking force.

Lucky Bill stood more lightly balanced and eyed his foe. He knew that there was more truth than fiction in this defiant speech, and by the method of Harry's advance he recognized a dangerous and new foeman. Yet he was undaunted. He had flipped his hat aside and stood with something akin to a smile of fierce pleasure.

The girl, watching him in wonder, knew that he was happy. He was a big man, taller than Landrie, and broad of shoulder, but compared to the compact bulk of the latter he seemed actually fragile. He remained now, his hands hanging at his sides, until Landrie came close. And then he sprang. Both hands drove out with the speed of snapping whiplashes, thudded into the blocking arms of Landrie, and then as the burly fellow struck in return Lucky swerved lightly away.

But as a circling wind keeps flinging a feather back and back into one's face, so Lucky whirled, and darting repeatedly, smashed with both hands at Landrie and was away again. She began to sympathize with Harry. It seemed that he was rooted to the ground, unable to reach this flying antagonist, and chained by his slowness, while the other hammered him with those smashing blows.

But presently, as Lucky darted in and out again, Landrie lowered his arms, and she saw that he was grinning.

"Every one a miss, Lucky," he said. "Ain't touched more'n my arms yet. You'd ought to go on the stage and be a dancer, son. As a fighter you ain't worth a damn!"

She saw that his face, indeed, was unmarked. He was not even panting, and she could plainly hear the labored breathing of Lucky. It was like watching a panther, terrible with tooth and claw, attack a bear again and again, unable to harm the rugged beast. But now Lucky, with a groan of rage at his own impotence, slipped in, and for the first time stood close, exchanging blows.

They fell in a rain; he was striking thrice for every

once that Harry Landrie used his fists. But still Harry was not driven back; and then she noted that while Lucky lashed out with his arms, swinging far back from his sides, Landrie was driving short punches inside the flailing arms of his foe, and every one of those punches racked and shook the gunfighter. Then the right shoulder of Harry Landrie lowered, settled, and his right fist landed high on the head of Lucky.

The latter was shot back, staggered, dropped upon one knee, and Landrie, with a shout, rushed at him. It was horrible, and yet fascinating to see. She pressed her hands above her heart and could not draw her eyes away while Lucky got reeling to his feet, wavered, and then steadied himself with a set jaw of determination. Harry Landrie, checking his rush abruptly as soon as he saw the other put himself into a posture of defense, dropped back once more behind his extended left arm, and began the former process of slowly stalking his enemy.

There was something wrong in all this, she felt. Harry Landrie unexpectedly was the one who had the superior strength and skill in this battle, and yet he was conservative, making his enemy take all the chances. And Lucky, ignorant of anything except to rush and strike wildly, flung himself again and again at the unshaken bulk of the other. It was like a gallant last hope; it was like a cavalry charge upon a fortress. For some reason her heart went out to the tall, agile fellow, who smiled as he battled.

Harry Landrie was beginning to relax his vigilance contemptuously.

"Look at him, Molly," he said with a sneer. "Look at the terror of the ranges bleeding like a stuck pig; and this ain't half of what I'm going to do to him."

54

She saw that what he said was true. Lucky was in profile, and she saw only his pallor and his smile. Now, dancing away, she caught a glimpse of his full face—the blood was running dark down the side of his face.

Suddenly her head spun; she became sick and weak and closed her eyes. When she opened them again Lucky had leaped in again.

She had seen wolves fight dogs. They fought as Lucky fought, a spring, a slash, and then away again. But this was the first time that she was able to guess the power of those flying arms of Lucky.

His left fist, as he leaped, crashed as usual into the blocking arms of Harry Landrie. But he had learned something by painful experience. This time he did not follow with a second blind blow of his right. He started the hand forward and checked it in midair. Molly saw the bulky left forearm of Landrie fly up to meet the blow and then down as the impact did not come; and as it came down, the right fist of Lucky lashed over and cracked with a sound like palms clapped together against the jaw of the burlier foeman.

Harry Landrie, caught plainly by surprise, staggered, struck out blindly. Then both fists of Lucky went home on the jaw of the other. Harry Landrie went down like a steer under the mallet.

She caught her breath, expecting Lucky to leap on the stunned antagonist; but to her astonishment the tall man stood back a couple of strides and waited, calmly wiping the blood from his face. No boasting. He waited without sign of triumph; and Landrie groaned, toppled forward on his arms, and then dragged himself slowly to his feet.

He came toward Lucky, reeling, his jaw set, his eyes

glazed. His whole manner was like that of a drunkard. Before him Lucky receded.

"You're done, Landrie," he said. "I can't hit you when you're like this. Give it up. You've fought hard, I'll tell a man!"

Landrie dropped his arms to his sides as though in acquiescence, but the moment Lucky turned his head, he threw himself forward and wrapped his arms around the other.

Hot blood rushed into the head of the girl.

"It isn't fair!" she cried. "Harry, you haven't played fair!"

Lucky was writhing away from the arms of his foe, snarling: "You tricky swine!"

But Harry Landrie clung in the clinch until his dazed head was clear once more; and when Lucky finally thrust himself away, the big man stepped in, raised on his toes, and drove an uppercut into the jaw of the gunfighter.

It sent Lucky toppling away; and Landrie snarled with pleasure.

Chapter Six

Foul Play

The same hot shame grew in the girl. Landrie was her champion, and Landrie had not played fair. She heard him gasping: "I'm going to kill you now, Lucky. I'm going to kill you!"

But Lucky was only temporarily stunned; he came in again, weaving like a will-o'-the-wisp. This time Landrie was prepared. The blows of his enemy glanced from his arms. He struck in return only once, a powerful jerking blow that thudded on the ribs of Lucky and sent him back, gasping.

So the fight went on. It was always Lucky who rushed; it was always Landrie who struck the decisive blow in the close fighting. He was beginning to follow up his advantages, too. He reminded her of some remorseless bulldog, untired by his efforts, slowly closing in on the foe. Lucky, leaping away from an unsuccessful attack, slipped on a stone, and tumbled to his knees; instantly Landrie balled his fist, and leaping on the other, felled him with a blow behind the ear. Lucky pitched on his face and lay limp. And Molly Aiken, with a cry of horror, ran in between them.

"You hit him when he was down. You played crooked, Harry! Stand away and let him get up again; he did that much for you!"

But he turned on her with a beastlike snarl and a wave of his big arm cast her staggering away to a distance. She was nothing to him now. He had gone mad with the taste of blood.

"I'll do better," he sneered. "I'll help him up. Get up, Lucky!" And he kicked the fallen man in the side.

The thud of the blow turned her sick; she closed her hand on the butt of one of the revolvers she held.

"Lucky!" she cried. "Get up!"

As if he feared the fallen man might answer that appeal, Landrie flung himself on the prostrate figure. His right arm crooked around the throat of Lucky, and under the strangling pressure Lucky's head snapped back. She saw for a terrible instant his contorted face.

Fear of death, however, seemed to have revived him. He began to struggle fiercely, with writhing legs; Landrie, changing his hold a little for a better grip, was toppled off his balance. The two dissolved into a whirl of tumbling bodies which ended with both springing to their feet.

Lucky began circling again, more crouched now; and something about him made the girl know that the battle had changed. It had been more or less of a game for a wager before; now the prize was life, and the loser would die. She knew not which one to think the more formidable. Harry Landrie had cunning, power, weight; and against this Lucky opposed only a thing which she could not name. A flamelike quality. Just as he had revived from a stupor to fight desperately and come away alive, so she felt that he could again rise to any emergency.

Harry Landrie, standing with feet braced, was turning slowly to keep his face to the man who stalked him, raining curses; but Lucky answered never a syllable. Only, when the moon fell full on his face, her blood went cold.

She heard the beat of the hooves of many horses on the other side of the hill. One cry would bring them to her and end this grim battle. But what would happen to Lucky Bill then? She knew the temper of her father too well, and the temper of all those rough cowpunchers who adored the ground she walked on. They would have a noose around Lucky's neck in ten seconds. Besides, she could not have cried out if she had wished to do so. She had no power except to stand there, breathless, fascinated, watching the powerful bodies of those men and their set faces.

Harry Landrie was no longer a man. He was a beast. But there was something glorious in the battling of the other.

He leaped again. Truly he had learned much. While his fists lashed into the face of Landrie he was weaving his body from side to side, and the straight, driving blows of Landrie missed him altogether, or else harmlessly glanced from his shoulders and the sides of his head. Blood burst out from the cheekbone of Landrie; from a gash beneath his eye. He went back, carried by a literal shower of heavy blows, striking out desperately and vainly at that wavering foreman. Then, planting himself firmly, he struck up a quick, short blow. It landed fair and square on the end of Lucky's chin and rolled him back on his heels.

Yet before Landrie could reach him he had recovered his balance and was attacking again. But once more that ugly uppercut shot under his guard, up, and sent him reeling away.

A frenzy seized the girl, and the name of that blow to which Lucky seemed to be blind came to her.

"It's an uppercut, Lucky. Keep farther away. An uppercut."

"You witch!" shouted Landrie. "I'll beat him in spite of you." And he charged to finish the battle.

Still there remained in Lucky that springlike power to recoil and strike when he seemed most helpless. A blow to his body doubled him; a blow to the forehead jerked him upright again. Landrie, with a yell of exultation, whipped back his pile-driver right hand and poised himself for the finishing blow. Then Lucky, lunging weakly forward, struck overhand, and by chance the fist lodged on the chin of Landrie.

It was not enough to break the skin; it did not even make the big man shake his head; but it cost him his balance, and before he could set himself for a second time, Lucky was out of range, with a head cleared once more. The weaving assault began for the third time.

Again that deadly, slashing shower that was cutting Landrie to ribbons bore him back. Again he set himself.

"His right hand. The uppercut!" cried Molly Aiken.

She saw that she was heard. The elbow of Lucky dropped, and the lifting fist of Landrie met it. He yelled with the pain, threw himself back for a mighty blow. Under his arms sprang Lucky, like a wolf, and the long, straight punches cracked twice on the jaw of the burly man. His arms sagged down; his head fell; he lunged blindly forward, and pitched upon his face. The head recoiled a little from the ground. And then he lay without quivering.

"I've won," said Lucky Bill thickly. "You—come—with me!"

She neither saw nor heard him clearly. She was only vaguely aware that he was sinking down on the side of the hill, unnerved. What filled her mind was the limp body of Harry Landrie, and something odd and horrible in the way his legs lay, twisted together, and the position of his right arm, flung out as though it were broken at the shoulder.

She ran to him, lifted with all her might. It seemed marvelous that that prodigious weight of fighting muscle directed by a cunning mind had been made helpless, inert, by a single blow. She tugged, and the body rolled heavily over.

It was as she had guessed. There was a deep red gash in the center of Landrie's forehead. She kneeled beside him, tore open his shirt, felt for the heart. There was a quiver that made her breathe one brief prayer. She let her hand rest a moment longer to be sure. There was no response. She dug the tips of her fingers into the flesh, as though she would force the life to return.

Still there was no response. Looking into the face something about the expression of the open eyes convinced her. Landrie was dead.

"Lucky!" she moaned. "Lucky! He's dead! Dead!"

But Lucky did not answer.

She saw that he sat against a rock with his head fallen, his arms dangling feebly beside him. She ran to him and lifted his head between her hands. It rolled feebly back, and the dull eyes looked up at her, bewildered.

Of the two young giants who had battled there for her, one was dead; the other was for the moment helpless as a child.

In that instant that the weight of Lucky's head pressed against her hands Molly Aiken lived longer than all the years of her life. A new light came to her, came on her, and she saw herself as she was. What she had felt before to be natural and praiseworthy pride now showed as sullen selfishness. The spirit that had balked and thwarted her father all her life had now worked to completion and had killed a strong man.

What was she to be worth this struggle? Was her face a virtue? What was her value in the world? What could she give to replace even Harry Landrie? Even the victory of Lucky and his danger and labor were for nothing. She knew now and frankly admitted to herself that she had never intended to marry Mat Morgan. She would never have dreamed of it except to irritate her father. Yet Lucky had come on this mission, had risked his own life and taken the life of another man for the sake of that whim.

That danger was not all. What would the world say? That Harry Landrie had been killed while vainly trying to keep a professional gunfighter from carrying away a young girl. She knew what that would mean in the mountain desert. Lucky Bill would never dare show his face again where men assembled. He would be taboo. The very children would arm themselves against him.

The name which, in spite of its danger, had been

clothed with a sort of a glory through the length of the mountain desert would now be covered with shame and infamy. By tomorrow he would be outlawed. A price would be on his head. A dog would have more rights than he whom she had just now seen fighting so fairly, so chivalrously, and for a prize in which he had no personal interest.

They would hound him down. How long he might last she could not dream; but sooner or later—she had often heard her father say it—every outlaw came in the end to his recompense, and that was a dog's death, unpitied.

She lifted her white face to the moon.

"Oh, God," sobbed Molly Aiken, "teach me how to save him!"

She pressed her hands against the thick-muscled shoulders—they were shuddering as if in an ague—and forced him back against the ground. With her handkerchief she wiped the blood from the cut on his face. She opened his shirt; at the first breath of the night air he recovered rapidly, and lifted himself on one arm.

"It's done?" he asked.

"It's over."

He stood up and saw the motionless form of Harry Landrie, the arms flung wide, the eyes open, and the red gash on the forehead.

"What happened? That ain't my work!"

She stood watching him miserably; her silence was the assent; and now she heard again the rattling hooves of the horses of her father's men as they came back across the hills, vainly hunting for some clue to the trail of the fugitives. This dead man, sooner or later, they would be sure to find. And then?

"We've got to go. Quick!"

"It was an accident," said Lucky. "I didn't mean that!"

"Ah, yes, Lucky. An accident! But who would believe it? Ten men couldn't swear you out of it. There's the stone with the blood on it. They'll say you struck him down with that. Lucky, seconds count!"

They got to their saddles of one accord and headed on up the cattle trail. Over the next hill, onto a broad level—then a shout went tingling up behind them. It seemed very close, but that was because many voices were joined in one.

"Is your horse in shape for good running?" asked the girl.

"He's sound. Wind isn't touched yet."

"Then let him go. You hear?"

"They've found Landrie's body? I'll go back and explain somehow. You keep on—"

"Go back? That would be suicide. I know my father. He'd have a rope around your neck in two minutes. Only a run can save you, Lucky. Or here—take my horse. He's full of running. I'll go back and try to throw them off."

"Let you go back?" Lucky grinned mirthlessly at her. "I've paid a price for you, lady. You stay with me. Keep right ahead in the trail, and feed your hoss the spur. Now, go!"

She obeyed without a word. After all, it was true. She could not deny the price of blood, and in some way she felt that the man had established a claim upon her. She loosed the reins, touched her mount with the rowel, and they flew at a full gallop through the hills.

It was well for Lucky that he had a guide with him

who knew a country that was strange to him. She picked her own way, sometimes taking shortcuts over steep grades, sometimes swerving aside from the rough going into smooth-bellied swales, and they drove steadily north.

Behind them the pursuit first spread out fanlike. They heard voices shouting to the right and the left of them, far back; but presently these sounds drew together in the center; from a hilltop behind them came a yell, and looking back they saw the horses of the cowpunchers streaming over the crest. Molly Aiken looked back, cried out in fear, and then leaned over the mane of her horse and shot him out to full speed.

That sight stunned Lucky Bill. It was as if the girl actually did not wish to be taken by her father's men. When he could rally from his surprise he called her back to a slower pace. She obeyed, wondering. She thought at first, horrified, that he would attempt to drive off the pursuit with snapshots to the rear, but he rode without ever turning his head and kept his mustang well within its strength. In the meantime the cowpunchers, with the goal in full sight in the moonlight, were riding like mad, flailing with quirts, swinging their hats like a wild party riding into a peaceful town.

They ate up the ground between; the level going gave to choppy ups and downs through the hills. What was happening? Was Lucky going to give up? And then came the words:

"Now faster, faster yet! That'll do. Steady'"

She had her mustang just inside a dead run through that dangerous ground, and now she saw the effects of Lucky's maneuvering, for the cowpunchers dropped farther and farther back. They had already used up their

65

mounts pretty well in the scurrying back and forth to pick up the trail. The race to take the fugitives when they were once in view had thoroughly winded the ponies.

The rancher and his men were in the position of jockeys who, having ridden at full speed for two miles, find themselves at the end of that distance confronted with a long chase; while Lucky and the girl, rating their horses well inside their strength, stretched out a rapidly widening gap. The pursuers hit the choppy ground, and their mustangs, fagged by the hard pace, began to flounder and miss. Far behind her Molly Aiken heard the noise of voices, the cursing, the shouts to the horses, die off into a murmur, revived now and then when the wind picked it up.

By that time Lucky's horse, tired by his long labors of that night, was running heavily, but the big rider kept him steadily to that gait until they broke out on a high ridge of the hills. He called for a halt here and ranged up beside the girl. Looking down, she saw a broad sweep of country. The far hills were jet-black, but pale moonshine lay over the country at their feet with four patches of darkness near and far—ranch houses. She found that her companion was looking not at what lay before them, but steadily at her.

"Lady," he said at length, "I got this to say: You've played square. I didn't think it could be done. Asking your pardon, I never knew a girl could stick by the rules of the game. You didn't make no move against me when I was fighting Landrie—matter of fact, it was what you said that showed me how to beat him."

"Because he fought like a cowardly sneak, Lucky!"

"Hush," murmured the big man, raising his hand. "Landrie is dead."

For the first time in her life Molly Aiken was placed in a predicament where her tongue failed her. She could only stare at the gunfighter. And yet, oddly, she did not resent it. She felt very much as when Father Connell corrected her with his gentle voice.

He was speaking again, praising her: "And when they started chasing us, you didn't try to get away. You could of done it. Why didn't you?"

Once more she could not speak. A tumult of words came up to her lips, but remained unspoken. She wanted to tell him that, knowing the doom which was about to fall on him, knowing that it had been accomplished for her sake, she was filled with a great, vague desire to help him—how she could help she could not tell. It was that fear that she might seem childish that kept her silent. She only said, at last: "I don't know why I kept with you, Lucky."

He found a solution: "It's because you know I'm straight, and that I'm going to get you to Morgan, eh? You've stuck with me because I'm taking you to Mat?"

How could she deny it? As a matter of fact, Mat was not in the remotest corner of her brain.

"It's because I've forgotten about my own affairs for a little, Lucky. Do you think that I've forgotten that for my sake—for Mat's sake, I mean—you've killed a man? Do you think I can forget that, Lucky?"

"But that's the very thing you got to forget. It's nothing. What's the life or the death of one man compared with a big thing? And the big thing is the way you love Mat Morgan." He sighed. "It means a pile—a thing like that. I didn't know a girl could do it—give up the kind of a home you're giving up, and go out to foller a gent like Mat, that's got nothing except the saddle he rides in. Look here!''

She was forced to lift her face. She saw the dark scar on his cheek; she saw him transfigured with emotion. ''What you've done for Mat,'' he said, ''is the sort of thing that don't die. It keeps on living. A mighty long time from now folks will be telling their little girls how you cut away and gave up everything for the sake of the man you loved. Look at what it means just to me! It puts every woman I'll ever meet one step up. I'll take off my hat to 'em the same's I take off my hat to you.''

The big, flopping hat came off in his hand. She saw the moon glinting on his hair, and a light of another sort in his eyes. Her head bowed miserably. But how could she deny it? Could she tell him that one man had died for the sake of her whim? That he himself was in peril for the sake of the same heartless fancy?

Shame took hold on Molly Aiken—not hot shame, but the cold that goes to the heart of a man. He had put on his hat again and was sweeping the country that lay below them.

''We've got to get where I can change hosses. This one is played out. D'you know any of them ranches? Which is the most likely for us to go to? Which will ask the fewest questions?''

She told him briefly.

''Over yonder is the Lewis house. The Lewis boys are running it now. But they are pretty talky. Like as not they wouldn't trade or sell a horse unless they knew you. Then there's the Patterson place—the nearest one straight down in the hollow. They are poor folks. I don't think they have a horse that's worth riding, Lucky. Over to the right—you can just make it out—is the place where the Lesters live—''

"Was Jerry Lester among 'em?" he cut in.

"Yes."

"Then leave them out. If Jerry saw me hunting for a quick change of hosses in the middle of the night he'd be sure something was up."

"There's only one left."

"Then we'll try that one."

"They're the Tompkins, though. You can see the house beyond that hill. They have horses, and you could get one easily from them. The trouble is, they have too many horses. The first place dad will take his men is to the Tompkins place to get remounts and keep on our trail. And if we've just left, the Tompkins will know the direction we've started in."

"It's better than nothing. That way, then. No other place we could drop in at?"

"The haunted house—that's the only one."

"Haunted house?"

"But why is there such a desperate hurry? I think dad has given up the trail."

"He hasn't. He's rated his hosses off our pace, that's all. But he'll keep bulldogging it along, and before morning he'd catch me with this tired skate of mine. Listen!"

She canted her head. Far away, sure enough, she heard a murmur coming up the wind.

Chapter Seven

The Haunted House

"But what about that there haunted house?"

"Have we time to talk?"

"We'll jog on slow. Sounds interesting to me."

Over the creaking of the stirrup leathers and the grunting of the horses, she told him.

As early as she could remember, that old house had been up there in the canyon, a place surrounded by superstitious reverence and inhabited by one old white man and one old negro. It was close to the railroad, but no vagrant ever came that way. Rumor had it that the old fellow never allowed man, woman, or child to cross his threshold.

Once there had been a full family there—but the family had dissolved in the first generation of the early settlers of this country, and the old white man was the last of the race, to all appearances. How he lived no one could tell. His ranch buildings had disintegrated; his ranges had been sold; his herd of cattle was reduced to a miserable sweeping of strays. Yet now and again he drifted into Wheeler—more often the old negro went in and made the purchases. The whole town turned out to see him.

Of late years the solitary had never showed his face. And since he did not come to Wheeler, no man came to his ruinous ranch. It was dangerous to do so. In time past the semiphilanthropic gossips had tried to get into the wrecked house. If they insisted too far they were met with powder and lead. A door would fly open; there would be a flash of a thin old face, surrounded with white hair; and then a rifle held to the shoulder with steady hands.

Vagrants, who learn to follow the trails to easy meals by sure signs, avoided the house of the solitary as if the air were poisoned.

"But he's a living man, anyway," said Lucky. "Why do they call it the haunted house?"

"Because he's more like a ghost than a man, I guess. Besides, some say that he's a hundred years old. I guess that isn't true. But old Taliaferro—"

"What?"

"Taliaferro is his name. Do you know the family, maybe, or some relation?"

He had started violently.

"I think maybe—no, I guess not. Taliaferro?"

A moment of silence.

"That's where we're going—to the haunted house."

"Lucky!"

"Why not?"

"But he has no horses. Nothing but some old mules for his broken-down buckboard."

"We'll do without horses. We'll stay there till your father has had a chance to go on by. Then we'll start again tomorrow all fresh."

"But you can never get in. He's merciless as a wild dog, they say."

"No man is as bad as all that. I figure it's mostly talk. Anyway, it's worth trying. They'll never think of looking for us there."

"But if they did come there you'd be lost. The haunted house is in a blind valley, Lucky, and they would block the mouth of it."

"All the more reason that they'll never look for me there. Last place a man hunts for his hat is on the hat-tree. Now, full speed!"

They sent their horses into a strong gallop, straight across the wide valley, and up the farther slope until the wall of hills gave back and broke up into a number of gorges running into the heart of the range—and down one of these the girl guided them until Lucky saw in the shadows the outlines of a group of buildings. The first glance showed ample excuse for the epithet "haunted."

Against a background of tumbled sheds, barns, and stables the weight of whose roofs had at length proven too great for the rotten supports, with a scattering of second-growth forest sweeping away toward the hills on every side—in such a setting rose a great square-shouldered house whose windows were black and empty squares; and at one corner a lonely tower went up a story and a half above the rest of the structure.

The pale moon was over this gloomy ruin, covering the details of damage, so that nothing showed clearly except the emptiness of those windows and their eyelike quality—and one end of the long front veranda utterly collapsed.

Even Lucky Bill was daunted, and the girl was almost afraid to be left alone in the shrubbery near the house. He reassured her briefly, and, leaving her concealed, went to the front of the house, crossed the veranda, which groaned and shrieked under his weight, and struck his fist against the door. It shook and rattled under the blow.

Listening, he heard the faint echo go through the house—no other answer. He knocked heavily on the door again, and this time the echo was a dull and rumbling thunder that rolled away into the distant interior.

At last he heard a step descending stairs. He could tell, not by the wholesome thudding of feet, but by a light squeaking that journeyed down out of the upper regions, and then came more and more lightly toward the door. It paused for a moment there.

Lucky noted that no ray of light had fallen through the myriad little cracks which seamed the door. The inhabitant must have felt his way in the absolute dark of the interior. It was more ghostly than Lucky would admit even to himself. He shook away this fear resolutely, and raised his voice.

"Open up, partner. I'm stalled here for the night."

There was a solemn pause. Then a deep, strong throat rolled out the answer: "Sir, this is no crossroads tavern. Ride on to the town."

"How far is it to the town?"

"I have never noticed. Good night."

Lucky caught the handle of the door. It shook and creaked under his energetic shaking.

"If you don't turn the lock," he declared, furious, "I'll tear the damned door down. That's straight!"

"The lock," returned that deep, strong voice, "is not the only thing that will keep you from entering here."

The idea that any one should actually try to bluff him, Lucky Bill, made the hot blood rush to his head.

"You infernal old four-flusher!" he thundered. "Do you think I give a damn for your tricks and your ghosts? I tell you, I have to stay here for the night, and ten like you won't keep me out."

"Sir, I have never yet been accused of being a ghost."

"All right. I'll give the world first-class reasons for calling you a ghost unless you open up."

He could hear the man within clearing his throat.

"You threaten me," said the other, "like a man of imagination, at least. Who are you?"

"Bill is my name, and they's some call me Lucky."

"Lucky Bill? Your luck has brought you to the wrong stopping place for the night."

A frenzy of exasperation seized on Bill. He set his shoulder to the door with all his strength. It complained noisily, but did not yield.

"You may as well stop wasting your efforts," said the man within. "That door is oak. Time has told on it, but like some other things in this house it retains some strength."

"Partner," said Lucky through his teeth, "I warn you, if this door ain't opened freely I'll smash the lock with a bullet."

"Nonsense," replied the other coolly enough. "Nobody but a fool would make a burglar of himself for a night's lodging."

"I've got my gun in my hand. Stand clear of the door

or you may pick up the slug."

He waited. Eventually a deep-throated laughter rolled out at him.

"Impossible, Lucky Bill! You will not fire the shot. I am directly in line with the lock, and the bullet would enter my body."

Lucky was staggered by this astonishing assurance.

"Partner," he said solemnly, "say your prayers quick, then. By the time you count to ten a .45 slug goes through that lock."

"Very well. I am waiting patiently. I have come closer, you see? I am exactly in line with the lock, and the bullet cannot fail to strike me."

"It's on your own head, then. I've warned you fair and square."

He found mysteriously, that he could not press the trigger. It was as if another force pulled his finger out.

"I was never in less danger in my life," the man inside was saying.

"Confound you, what makes you so certain?"

"Because you're not phlegmatic enough to be a villain, my friend. Passionate men are men with a sense of humor, Lucky Bill, and men with a sense of humor do not commit murder to break into a house. You are finding now that you cannot shoot."

With a muttered oath Lucky dropped the gun back in the holster.

"You win," he said gloomily. "But it's a cheap gent that bets a full house against a pair of deuces. Good night, and be damned to you!"

He turned away, when he was stopped by the other calling: "Wait!"

He veered about.

"As far as food is concerned, I could give you some provision."

"That's nothing to do with it. I want shelter."

"No man, sir, has crossed the threshold of this house for fifteen years."

"Nor a woman either?"

"What! There is a woman with you?"

"There sure is."

There was a pause. At length: "I begin to feel, sir, that I have to do with a gentleman."

"You ain't, not the way you mean. You got to do with a cowpuncher."

"Occupations are accidents. Lucky Bill, stand back from the porch; stand back in the moonlight. I am going to open this door for the sake of seeing your face."

Rejoiced to see that affairs were at length turning in his favor, Lucky obeyed without a word.

"Furthermore, I'm armed, Lucky Bill. Keep that in mind."

The lock turned, grating, the door swung slowly ajar, and Lucky found himself staring into black vacancy. Not a living thing could be seen in the hall.

In that blackness a shadow took shape; there drew into view the lengthy barrel of an old rifle, and beside it, hardly so tall as his weapon, was a little old man huddled into a dressing gown. His body was lost in darkness. But owing to the quantities of white hair and the sharply trimmed, triangular beard, there seemed to be a peculiar light playing upon his face. His greeting was as startling as his appearance.

"Sir," said the deep, large voice which mated so ill with the withered figure, "I have missed you by three inches at least. You are over six feet?"

"I sure am."

"The presence of the lady completely alters matters. I could not have guessed that one was with you—by your earlier language."

Lucky smiled in spite of himself.

"She's on the other side of the house, waiting."

"Bring her here at once then."

So Lucky hurried around the house and came to Molly Aiken.

"The ghost ain't a ghost," he informed her. "It's a queer old gent that looks like a picture. Couldn't do a thing with him till he found out they was a girl with me."

She stopped short.

"When he finds I'm not your wife, traveling at this time of night—"

He knew that she was crimson, so he looked steadily straight before him.

"He's the sort of a gent that don't *think* about things like that. It's all right."

She started on again, more slowly. When they reached the front of the house she took his arm, and he looked down with astonishment at her hand.

"You're dead fagged, I guess," said Lucky. "We'll get you to bed in a minute."

He was suddenly conscious of his own size and strength and of her weakness. For some reason his mind leaped a gap and struck on the picture of Mat Morgan. It caused him a pang—why, he could not tell. They found Taliaferro had discarded his weapon and stood in front of the veranda with the moonlight flashing on his white hair. He wore it combed long, after an old school; it was as thick and fluffy as a wig.

"Mr. Taliaferro," said Lucky, "this is Miss Aiken."

It seemed to him that the dark, bright eyes of the old man flashed from the girl to him and back again, but it was a glance so swift that he could not be sure of it.

"My dear," said he, taking her hand, "I am happy to have you with me. Will you come in?"

They crossed the veranda. Mr. Taliaferro raised his head and sent a voice of thunder through the open door.

"George! The infernal old ruffian sleeps like the dead. George! Why I keep him I don't know. George! Lights! Habit is a terrible thing, Miss Aiken. It keeps me saddled with an incubus who used to be a servant. George! Men without spirit grow old. George has no spirit. *George*!"

At this fifth thundering repetition there was a stir and clattering in the upper part of the house, and presently a voice calling: "Marse Jeff'son! Yes, Marse Jeff'son. Coming, suh!"

They went carefully into the pitch-black hall, and now a flicker of light showed in the distance above them, and presently a lantern was brought into view. Him who carried it they could not make out except his white hair. For the rest, he was a distorted and gigantic shadow which strode wavering along the wall, coming slowly down to the lower level. But the lantern light showed more than its bearer.

It streamed first across the lofty ceiling of that hall. It was in itself a noble apartment, running up a height of two ordinary stories, and vaulted in what had once been a solid and pretentious manner. But the figured plaster had long since rotted and dried and cracked away. Here and there Lucky saw glimpses of complete designs in the yellow plaster—flying messengers with winged heels and shoulders, foliage, arabesques—but in other places

78

the material had fallen away and left the bare slatework to which it had been attached. Moreover, there was a liberal coating of dusty cobwebs.

The lantern descended and left this upper level in darkness as it was carried down the winding stair. Lucky saw the walls of the hall now. Here and there the light flashed dimly back from great mirrors, filmed with dust, cobwebbed in the corners. There were heads of animals whose eyes were still bright as with life—a desolate sight in this ruined place.

The light-bearer came on to the floor, and now the swinging lantern showed the flooring warped into waves, uncleaned for years it seemed. As the loose board stirred under the foot of George a faint mist of dust rose and was plainly visible before the lantern. The room was large, but the short steps of George made it seem illimitable as he came slowly toward them.

They could see him at length. Time had cramped his features and bunched them; the hand which held the bail of the lantern was withered as the claw of a bird; his bald head was fringed with tight curls, pure white; and the years had dimmed the original ebony to a sort of dusty gray. Coming close, he raised the lantern so that the light fell more fully upon the strangers, and in so doing he illumined his own face and his own buried eyes.

"George," said Mr. Taliaferro, "this is Miss Aiken, and this is—"

"Bill will do for me. I'm glad to meet you, George."

"Yes, suh."

"My friends are staying here tonight. You can lay out a little supper, George."

"No, if you please," said the girl. "I can't eat; I'm too tired for that."

"Why, then, you can see that her room is in order. Immediately, George."

But the little old negro was blinking, confused.

"Marse Jeff'son," he murmured faintly, "if I could see you a moment—"

"Confound it, where are your manners, George? One would think you had never been taught better."

It was strangely dreary to hear that mellow, young voice booming through the ruins of the house.

Lucky was staring, fascinated, when Molly Aiken touched his arm and drew him to one side.

"There's some trouble," she whispered. "Let George talk with his master."

George, in fact, immediately drew Taliaferro aside and began to pour out a whispered explanation with many gestures of distress. They heard old Taliaferro clearing his throat; his voice was as loud as ever.

"Nothing at all! Nothing at all!" He turned to them. "Miss Aiken, George tells me that the guest rooms are quite upset. Ha!" He paused, collected himself again, and seemed to dare Lucky Bill to smile. "As a matter of fact—the linen has been sent—"

"That's nothing, Mr. Taliaferro. I can roll up in a blanket; I'm used to roughing it."

"But the linen is not all—eh, George? Confound it, the rooms seem to be positively disordered, ah—bare, in fact. But you shall use my room, if you will. This way, Miss Aiken."

She protested in vain; he overruled her with a gesture, and gathering her arm under his he led her straightway toward the stairs. Molly Aiken, in her distress, even

80

turned back to Lucky, begging with a glance that he would intercede and convince the little old man that she would not deprive him of his bed.

George went on ahead with the lantern and Lucky followed, but Jefferson Taliaferro so arranged his monologue that Molly could neither complain nor remonstrate. For instance, steering her around an actual gap in the flooring where the rotten boards had been crushed in: "Men are animals, Miss Aiken," he said. "It is you women who lift us up. Here am I like a bear in a den never paying heed to my own house until a lady comes in it—George!"

"Marse Jeff'son?"

"You infernal old rascal, have this flooring repaired at once."

"Yes, Marse Jeff'son."

"Steady on these stairs, Miss Aiken. You see how the boards wabble under you? Confound it, as if they would give way at every step. And don't trust your hand to that banister. I positively won't insure it to you. Here we are at the landing at last. By Heaven, the hall is dark as a coffin! Miss Aiken, you are like a light in my house. I see things for the first time. This must be changed. George, you hear me? Tush, my dear girl, not a word. Plenty of places for me to sleep, but not one where I would have you put up. You must even make the best of my room as it is."

A door of extraordinary breadth and height was fitted into the end of the upper hall; this George now opened, and by the time the rest of the party was at hand he had lighted two lamps.

What they revealed came as a shock to Lucky. He could see only dimly, for the two lights were not nearly

81

enough to bring out all the details of the room. Where the walls stepped out of the shadow they were a clean cream color, spotted here and there with the dark frames of pictures. On the floor, a richly colored carpet; to one side, a great four-poster with solemn curtains. It was like stepping through a wall into a new house to see this room. Molly Aiken looked on it in amazement. And Jefferson Taliaferro turned from one to the other and drank deep of their surprise.

Then he began to give a swirl of directions to George. Before Lucky knew well what had happened Molly Aiken, looking small and white of face with weariness, had smiled and waved good night, and the door closed behind Taliaferro. He had lighted a candle to guide the way downstairs again. Now he turned his hand about the flame so that the light shone upon the face of Lucky Bill alone.

Taliaferro kept himself in shadow for the sake of this scrutiny for several seconds; and then without a word of explanation or invitation to Lucky, he went past him down the hall, leaving him to follow or not as he chose.

Chapter Eight

The Hidden Room

There being no second choice, Lucky followed down the hall and down the stairs; when they reached the lower level the old man turned abruptly on him, and after looking sharply at him—for this seemed his habit before speaking—he asked Lucky if he were hungry.

"As a wolf," said the cowpuncher; "but the horses come first. Where can I put 'em up?"

At this Jefferson Taliaferro dropped into thought for a moment. At length, still without speaking, he led the way back through the house, through room after room, empty, ragged, dusty, and at the back porch lighted a second lantern and went with Lucky to the horses. He showed him to a shed where two mules were already tethered, miserable, bony creatures, and indicated by pointing where he could tie the two horses and where he could find provender for them.

Not once did he speak while Lucky unsaddled the animals and shook hay into their mangers, and when these preparations were completed he led the way back again to the house.

This time he brought his guest into the kitchen.

Of all the dilapidated apartments in that ruined house there was nothing to compare with the kitchen. It was under a shed roof built out at the rear of the house, and since the ceiling and the roof itself had long since been honeycombed by weather and years, it had been reenforced by heavy canvas. And this smoke-blackened canvas sagged down here and there, a home for rats who scampered and squealed above the heads of Lucky and Taliaferro.

The stove was of gigantic size, but it was a rusted wreck. From the big cupboard at one side the door had fallen and had never been replaced. Against the walls, barrels and boxes, all apparently of great age, were piled. Among these the old man rummaged rather vaguely and at length brought out to the eyes of Lucky a ham bone to which a red fragment of meat adhered, a can of coffee, and a tin of crackers. He assembled these things on the table and then stood looking in some embarrassment from them to his guest.

"George is apparently still busy with the room, sir. Perhaps you can cook for yourself? I, unluckily, have not the art."

Lucky Bill assented with the utmost good grace; in a moment he had ham frying and coffee simmering; had found plates and knives and forks and set out two places at the table.

"But I am not hungry," protested Jefferson Taliaferro.

"That ain't the point," grinned Lucky. "I don't like a sob part when they's a company around I can ring in. I'll tell you what I've done: I've gone hungry all day, rushing for a town where I could look somebody in the eye while I swung a fork. Eating alone is bad, and drinking alone is plain poison. Sit down, Mr. Taliaferro."

The old man obeyed. He even helped himself to a bit of the ham, and made an elaborate pretense of eating it, while Lucky rapidly swept a plate clear, and at the same time kept up a running fire of talk. His host watched him, nodding in silence at each period in the talk. Lucky got the impression that he was being looked at as from a distance.

"You come from the north, I guess?" said the old man at length.

"North. Murray City, to begin with."

So saying, Lucky glanced quickly at his host and away again. The old man had narrowed his eyes, looking into space, so that his brows lifted at the outside and gave his face an expression of rather satanic intelligence.

"Murray City?" he repeated. "There was a Taliaferro there, I think. But he spelled his name 'Tolliver.' "

"A different spelling, but the sound of it's the same," said Lucky.

"News comes slowly up this way," went on his host. "But some years ago we had tidings that Tolliver was killed?"

"Ten years ago—and your news right. He was killed."

The old man interlaced his fingers and nodded. After a time: "Bad blood will out like murder," he said.

"Just how do you mean that?" drawled Lucky.

"What I say, sir. Bad blood will out."

His eyes flared at Lucky, but the latter carefully avoided meeting them.

"There was no bad blood."

"Are you sure of that, young man?"

"As sure as I am that I'm sitting here. You'll be glad to hear it, I guess—you being the same name."

"Not the same name. Thank God he changed it, and made it different of his own volition. But years ago the name *was* the same. That was back—"

He stopped, as one who fears he has gone too far.

"In the South? Before the war?" said Lucky.

"Yes, before the war. Bad blood—yes, sir. And I understand that his neighbors at Murray City found him out at last and hunted him down?"

"It cost them three for one when they got him," remarked Lucky through his teeth.

"Yes, I think he gathered a little group of adherents around him and fought them off for a while? Well, he always had a smooth tongue."

Lucky Bill had either finished his meal or else he suddenly lost interest in eating. He pushed back from the table, folded his arms, and stared at the old fellow.

"Tolliver was a man," he said slowly.

"Tush! You are growing warm, my young friend."

"I was one of them that stood with him at the finish."

"You? Come! That was ten years ago."

"I was fifteen and big enough to handle a rifle.

"Why, no wonder you believe in Will Tolliver, then. The people we have served are the people we love; not what we get, but what we give—that's the bond between men. Well, sir, I'm not an iconoclast. But the truth will

86

out. I'll tell you the true story of Will Tolliver, and why he had to leave his home country. It was—"

"Wait," cut in Lucky. "I know that story. I've heard it a pile. It's hard-sounding yarn—what Tolliver done to the Harrison brothers, eh? But no matter how black it looked then and still looks, Tolliver was innocent."

"Sir, I lived within a mile of Tolliver when he committed that crime, and I know."

Lucky flushed and raised his fine head.

"Sir," he said, subtly mimicking the tone of the other in his younger voice, "Tolliver died in my arms, and I know! They ran him out of his home country and made him change his name because of a crime he never committed. He proved that he never committed it by the way he lived afterward. Twenty years of clean living.

"It was the old story that ruined him again. Two of the young Harrison boys came into Murray City. They found Tolliver was there and what his real name was— the real spelling, I mean. They spent their time going about talking. Tolliver was a proud man. When he heard what they were doing he went down to 'em and warned 'em to clear out of the town before he did 'em an injury. They wouldn't go. Instead, they got together a bunch of the boys who believed the rotten yarn they'd told and went out to call on Tolliver."

Lucky paused, gritting his teeth.

"They burned the house over his head; they burned his barns; he got away through the flames; they followed him. He picked up one or two friends and stood 'em off in a place in the hills. They didn't dare rush the old man They stayed at a distance and kept dropping slugs around us. Finally one got Tolliver through the body He fought till he couldn't stand; then he dropped. I tried

87

to pick him up. 'Billy,' he said, 'I'm done; but before you and God I ain't guilty; no, damn me if I am!' ''

"Tolliver's grammar was always poor," said the old man, but his eyes shone. "And what became of the rest of you?"

"Left us for dead. Two of the boys was. I come through alive, with only this to remember 'em by."

He touched his throat close to the collar. There was a great round white scar.

"There you are," nodded Taliaferro. "You fought for a man and spilled your blood for him, and therefore you're convinced that he was innocent. What we give is what makes us; not what we get."

"Sir," said Lucky, "there never was a crooked gent yet that could make a square shooter fight for him and die for him without no reward."

"A broad statement for a very young man, sir."

"Them's the things that a gent knows when he's born and can't learn afterward."

"Ha? You interest me, Mr.—"

"Bill is the name, I think I've said."

It seemed that Taliaferro was disappointed in being turned from his goal by this retort. He went on, however, with gathering intenseness: "And you're willing to swear by Tolliver, I take it? All because he talked openly to you, flattered you a little, joked with you? Those are the things that determine our opinions."

Lucky squirmed under this arraignment; he was growing excited. "I'll tell you, Mr. Taliaferro. You make up your mind about a man by the look of his eye and the grip of his hand and the sound of his voice. And in a hundred years you can't learn any more than you learn in the first hundred seconds. It ain't what a man says as much as it is what his eyes says at the same time.

"Look at you, now. You been smiling at me while I been talking about Tolliver. You been smiling in a way that would of made me a pile riled up if you was a young gent. But behind your smile you're dead serious. No matter what you been saying, d'you want me to tell you what's been going on inside your head?"

He leaned toward the old man, and the latter stiffened in his chair, looking at Lucky with something approaching fear.

"Inside your head, sir, you're saying: 'What Lucky Bill says is straight; and Tolliver was a clean man!' Talk up, and tell me I'm right."

Plainly, the old fellow was staggered; but though he blinked at this direct charge he quickly reassumed his former calm.

"The right of a young man is enthusiasm," he declared. "I like to see it. Also, a certain amount of faith in other men. At your age it's as necessary as love of country. Very necessary. It reminds me—" He stopped abruptly, for Lucky had stifled a yawn.

"Sir," he said solemnly, "I must tell you the truth at once. Aside from the cot on which George sleeps, my bed is the only one in the house. We must sit up the rest of the night—and you're weary."

He flushed while he made this admission so bluntly. It was the bluntness of pride, Lucky knew, and he waved the embarrassing situation to a great distance.

"Sleep is a plumb waste of time," he declared. "Every time I wake up I got a grudge for having lost so much of my life. Here's where you and me save a night from being lost, Mr. Taliaferro."

For the first time there was a faint wrinkling about

the eyes of the old man and a change of expression which, if it was not an outright smile, was certainly its equivalent.

"We'll find a better room to sit in, then," he said, and led the way out of the kitchen and into the right wing of the house.

Fumbling in his pocket he found a key, inserted it in the lock, and while he fumbled for the catch he looked back over his shoulder, half studiously, half wistfully, at Lucky Bill; as a child will when it is about to introduce an elder to a cherished treasure and is half in fear of being laughed at for the trouble. At length, however, Taliaferro turned the lock, resolutely threw open the door, and with a gesture of apology for entering the darkness first, stepped inside.

As for Lucky, he was beginning to be accustomed to strange things in this house, and he was not surprised that out of the very darkness of this room there rolled a new atmosphere. An odor, and yet it was not an odor. A match scraped, spurted a small, blue light—then a lamp flickered, and glowed into a steady light. He passed the doorway and stood entranced with what he saw.

Chapter Nine

Father Connell

Of all the men who rode with Henry Aiken on the trail of his lost daughter that night, there was only one who talked much, and this was a little half-breed from Canada who kept clamoring: "I seen him, and I knowed him—it's Lucky Bill! It's Lucky Bill! Don't press him too close, boys. And when you shoot, shoot straight!"

He had a shrill little voice, and he would keep up his singsong by the minute, in rhythm with the gallop of his horse. He had been one of the foremost in that spurt across the open which had almost brought them up with the fugitives, and which had incidentally winded their horses so they were hopelessly out of the race thereafter.

Henry Aiken was able to recognize the foolishness of this maneuver, but he was too proud to admit it openly, and the rest of the men were by no means courageous enough to call his mistakes to his mind. But they were a grim-minded lot as they spurred their horses through the moon haze.

In the first place, they wanted a death on account of the girl; for whether they had been a long time or a short time on the trail, they knew Molly Aiken and loved her, each in his own way. Besides, they had seen one dead man on that trail, and one glance at death hardens the mind.

They kept their thoughts to themselves. Henry Aiken had informed them briefly of the reward that they would have—the man who fired the shot that brought down Lucky Bill—and the reward that all the others would have for riding in that pursuit. They had no need of a reward, but the offer edged the metal and made them cutting blades.

Henry Aiken kept the lead as much by virtue of command as by his superior horse; but close beside him rode another man, a squat figure, with a long, black, deep-skirted coat. It was to him that Aiken spoke after they had ranged up and down the valley, after they had visited the ranch houses and heard no tidings of the fugitives.

"Father Connell, the next place is Wheeler. I'm going to get this fellow outlawed and have the sheriff on the trail."

The priest lifted his hat and wiped his forehead. He had accommodated the dignity of his office to the needs of his vast parish, and those needs had hardened him into a wiry horseman, yet he was hot and tired from the long ride. The moon was sufficiently bright now to show his square face, the wide, low forehead, deeply wrinkled between the eyes, and his sturdy jaw. They had made a pause by mutual assent on the top of a rise of ground, for their horses were nearly spent. The rest of the improvised posse had scattered here and there, waiting in silence for the word to resume the ride.

"Have you thought of what outlawry means?" asked the priest. "Every man's hand against one man—the law against whosoever gives him shelter except by compulsion—the rights of a dog, no, not the rights of a wolf; for a bounty is offered for his head. Think of it! For outlawry is the one legal way of turning a human being into a beast."

"Have you thought of what Lucky Bill is?" answered the rancher hotly. "And have you thought of what he's done tonight?"

"Do you think," said the priest quietly, "that he could have carried away Molly if she had been entirely unwilling to go with him?"

"Bah!" groaned Henry Aiken. "You know that girl. No reason in her. The way to make her do a thing is to command the opposite. The way to make her go through a gate is to put a lock on it. This dare-devil came along; he was something new, something different. She went with him, by the Lord, simply to spite me. And now she's lost!"

"Lost?"

"This is a clean country, Father Connell, but even in this country a girl can't go on all-night trips with a man without losing her reputation."

The priest raised his hand forbiddingly. "You are her father," he said sternly. "But even you have no right to speak one syllable of what you have spoken. I tell you this: I would trust her more a thousand miles away from me than I would trust another in the surveillance of her family. Besides, men of violence are men of honor. It is strange, but true. I have seen a thousand times that those who are lions among men are the lambs among women. Henry, I tell you from my heart that she is safe!''

The rancher was too deeply moved to answer. He found the hand of his companion and crushed it with a great grip. At length he said shortly:

''God help her! But whether it takes the rest of my life and the last cent of my money, this fellow is going to pay me for every step of this ride we've made tonight. Let's go on.''

''One last word. Give up violence, Henry. You have said yourself that violence is a whip that drives Molly in the opposite direction. Give up violence. Go back to your home. Trust this affair to a stronger power than yours or mine. My dear friend, you have to do with the heart of a woman, and the law has no power over that!''

It was like talking to an ear of stone. A moment later Aiken had set his group in motion, and they trotted slowly down the west road for the town of Wheeler. The sun was high before they reached that little village. It seemed to be drowsing in the sun, but at the coming of the weary riders it wakened into a new life. Henry Aiken went for the home of the sheriff, Jud Nevil; the cowpunchers made straight for the two saloons; and the priest, having looked to his horse, put his hands behind his back and walked by himself.

He was full of trouble, this good man. His work had been to a certain degree distinguished; his character was known in his church; he could have attained rapid advancement if he chose to leave the mountain desert for more populous fields. But his heart was there in the mountains and with the people of the mountains.

Above all, he had given greatly of himself to the making of the mind of Molly Aiken. Of all his works, she was the one in whom his influence was least easily discernible, and yet she was the one of whom he was most proud. She represented a continual battle through years. And since he had fought for her, he loved her.

It had been for her sake that he had come to the house of Aiken, and for her sake he had joined the hunt. What he was thinking of now was not so much the peril of Molly Aiken herself as of the future conflict between her and her father. Just now the rancher was occupied mostly with fears for the girl; when those fears were relieved, as the priest was certain they would eventually be, all the hot wrath in the nature of Aiken would be poured forth upon the head of the girl.

She would never endure a single word of rebuke. For one thing the good priest reproached himself—that he had never taught the rancher how best he might control the girl. It was not by compelling her with opposites; it was by winning her sympathy, her enthusiasm.

He himself had learned how to step into her mind, and once inside the guards it was the simplest matter to win her over. If she dropped a hard word, a half hour of patience would bring her almost on her knees in repentance. If a word of blame made her rise in rebellion, a moment of silence would make her writhe as if under a whip. Father Connell could wind her about his finger as easily as a skein of yarn; but he had taken a peculiar pride in his influence; he had guarded his secrets of management jealously, and now he was heaping blame on his own head for all that had happened.

In that mood he had wandered in what direction he knew not, among the houses and behind them, when he heard a sound like a rapid clapping of hands, not over-loud, but singularly heavy. It stopped him. Then it made him hurry on with an awakened curiosity until he had come around the side of a barn. Behind it he found the source of the noise—two boys, fighting with set teeth, in silence, and with a furious venom.

He was not a familiar of Wheeler, and consequently he knew the face of neither of them. Instead of rushing in between them now he leaned calmly against the corner of the barn and studied them with the most intense and silent interest. One might have thought him a pugilist criticizing the crude exhibition.

They were not well matched. One of the two stood inches taller and was many a pound heavier than his antagonist. He was, indeed, rather more youth than child. His hands and feet were larger than in proportion. He had man's boots on his feet, and his doubled fist was a formidable bunch of hard bones. Yet he was content to take the defensive, resting heavily back on his right foot and smashing out with all his power when the smaller boys came within range. He fought, indeed, like one half afraid, and the cause of his fear was not hard to find.

For the face of the little chap was convulsed with rage. Another boy, with that expression, would have been sobbing with fury, but this one spent his entire fury in blows. With a man's vest swaying loosely around his body, a man's trousers cut off at the knees blowing around his legs, bare-shanked, barefoot, he darted with catlike agility around his more stolid opponent, leaping in again and again with a shower of blows.

The majority of these were warded off, most of the rest glanced harmlessly from shoulders and ribs, but a moment after Father Connell had taken his post as spectator the smaller boy ran under the guard of the other and thumped him heavily in the stomach.

It doubled the other over like a closing jackknife, and as he bent he was met with a fusillade of blows to the face. One of them lodged solidly, and he rolled heavily to the ground. There he lay with both arms clasped around his stomach, writhing, gasping for breath.

The conqueror wasted no time in exultation. He flicked a thread of blood from his bruised lips and was instantly on his knees slapping the other on the back to bring back his wind. This was finally accomplished; the vanquished came panting to a sitting posture. He stared at his enemy as though he were too much astonished to feel pain.

"Well, Bud," he gasped, "you done it, right enough."

"It ain't worth talking about," said the other generously. "Thing was, Harry, you just naturally kept your guard too high. I kept hammering away at your head till you had your arms away up and it left your stomach plain open. If it wasn't for that, I guess you'd 've beat me, Harry."

Harry shook his head. "You sure can fight, Bud," he said.

Bud shifted from foot to foot, embarrassed by the praise.

"We just had to have it out," he said, "you being a new boy in Wheeler. Are we friends?"

He held out his hand, but the other looked at it dubiously.

"I dunno," he said carefully. "Me being bigger'n you, I guess I'll get laughed at a pile."

"The first one that laughs, I'll bust him one in the

jaw,'' declared Bud fiercely. ''Tell you what, Harry, you fight fair and square, and I'd bust a boy that laughed at you. Besides, they ain't nobody going to find out that we fought and who won, less'n you tell. I'm mum, for one.''

Light broke upon the face of Harry. ''Maybe this'll make us sort of friends—pals, maybe,'' he suggested hopefully.

But the face of Bud grew dark.

''I don't play partners,'' he said solemnly. ''You look around Wheeler for a while, and you'll see that I ain't got any pals; I ain't got any home nor no folks, you see. I just kind of drift around. Nearest I got to a pal is Jud Nevil.''

''That's him that's the sheriff, ain't he?'' cried the other, astonished.

''Yep, and him and me are pretty thick. Well, so long, Harry, and—''

He broke off with an exclamation, for his eyes had fallen upon the motionless figure of the priest. Harry exclaimed in turn and started to his feet.

''Wait a minute,'' said Bud darkly. ''You and me'll have words with this gent.''

But Harry had no wish for words; the secret of the fight was now discovered, and he fled at once around the corner of the barn.

Chapter Ten

A Philosopher

"Look at that!" he said gloomily to the priest. "Him that was talking about being a pal with me, and now running away. Can you beat that? You can't!"

"Not very manly," assented Father Connell.

Bud dropped his hands upon his hips and surveyed the other soberly.

"First thing," he said, "you and me is going to have words. Maybe you're a preacher, or something like that?"

"Something like that, son."

"All right. You go around telling people what they'd ought to do, mostly?"

"I'm afraid that that's what a great deal of my work amounts to after all."

"Well, sir, if you know what's right, maybe you can

tell me how come you standing there like a—a eaves-dropper, I think they call it—while two gents was set-tling a little affair of their own in private?''

Father Connell swallowed a smile; he felt that the least sign of mirth would banish him to the outer dark-ness as far as this boy was concerned.

"I heard a noise and came here," he said. "I saw a good fight was going on and I stayed to enjoy it."

"Well," admitted the boy, "that sounds tolerably rea-sonable. But I didn't know you preachers liked fight-ing?''

"I don't think most of us do. But I'm an exception."

"Then you're laying up a sermon most like?''

"Most like."

"Look here, are you mocking me, maybe?''

"Never!''

The boy pondered him, the frown growing and less-ening on his forehead as he pried into the grave face of the priest.

"All right. Suppose you start a little explaining?''

"I thought I'd explained already."

"About how you happened here—but not about why you sort of lingered around when you seen me and him was talking private.''

Father Connell cast about in his mind. Let it be known that he was sorely tempted, but he resisted the whisper of evil and told the truth.

"My friend," he said, "I have no excuse. As a matter of fact I should have turned away when I heard you talking with Harry.''

At this the sunburned eyebrows of the boy quivered and raised. He stared hard at Father Connell, and to the honor of the man let it be said that he flushed deeply.

Then an embarrassing pause fell between them.

"A thing like that," said the boy thoughtfully, "is pretty hard to say."

"Yes, it is. But I feel a lot better for saying it, Bud."

"I suppose it is. Speaking personal, which I don't think I'd of been able to say it. I'd of tried to, but most like I'd of bluffed it out rather than admit it."

"That's because you're a fighter. You see, I'm a man of peace."

This confession made Bud frown again, and his brows gathered over his sharp scrutiny.

"You rate yourself pretty low," he said slowly. "But mostly a gent that talks soft acts hard. I figure you're a good deal of a man. Say, what's your name?"

"Connell is my name. Daniel Connell."

"Glad to know you. I'm Bud."

He thrust out a brown fist, and over it the large, blunt-fingered hand of the priest closed. "It's a pleasure to know you, Bud."

The latter set his teeth; when he finally extricated his fingers his eyes dropped down at them for an instant.

"You got quite a grip," he admitted frankly. "More'n I thought."

"Sorry if I squeezed your hand too hard."

"Too hard? Huh, that's nothing to a gent like me. You go to show that you can't tell the insides of a man by his outside."

"Who has told you that?"

"Told me? Nobody. I don't aim to go around saying over again what other folks has said. Do you?"

"I'm afraid I do. One man in particular. Sometimes it's useful and pleasant to remember what another man has said."

The boy considered this carefully.

"Well," he said, "you're right. And I got to admit that sometimes in a pinch the things that Jud Nevil has said pop into my head as fine and handy as a gun comes into your fingers in a fight."

The priest blinked.

"No doubt," he acquiesced hurriedly. "No doubt in the world."

He began to cough behind his hand, but hastily sobered himself, for the lynx eyes of the boy were yellow and bright with suspicion.

"Jud Nevil is the sheriff?"

"Yep. The best all-round man-killing, hell-busting sheriff that ever cleaned up Wheeler, take him all in all. He—"

Here Bud checked himself.

"Maybe I shouldn't talk like that to you," he said diplomatically. "You being a preacher, maybe cussing don't come natural to you."

"Not exactly. But I don't very much mind. Talk just as you feel like talking, Bud. Curses which strike no deeper than the lips are not curses, after all, I imagine."

This explanation was a stickler for Bud. His eyes went wild and wandered for a moment as he groped after the meaning of the priest's words; then light suddenly dawned on him.

"You're right, sir. Yep, you're dead right. They's two ways of cussing. They's old Daddy Benton. He cusses away all day and it don't mean no more'n the yipping of a coyote jest talking to himself off in the hills. But when Gus Shaler twists up his mouth and says just plain 'damn,' it chases a chill up your back—like a fighting dog had just sniffed at your leg."

He mused, nodding contentedly as the truth of the observation filtered home in him.

"You're tolerable pleasant to talk to, Connell."

"As a rule the boys call me 'Father' Connell."

"You don't say! That's queer."

"It's because of the work I do."

"Lemme hear what that is, will you?"

"Of course. My work—well, it's to bring God closer to men."

"Huh?" grunted Bud. "You being tolerable close to Him yourself. I guess?"

"Not that. No, not at all. But I spend quite a little time thinking about Him, and I work for Him, you see?"

"Kind of. He's your boss, I take it?"

"Exactly. You couldn't define it better."

"I been hearing a pile of noise in the Empire," said Bud. "Let's go around and see what's happened."

"I can tell you, Bud. Lucky Bill has killed a man, and from this day forth he'll be an outlawed man."

Bud stopped short.

"Lucky Bill?" he whispered with bright eyes. "That *is* news. Wasn't it a fair break with the guns? Have they got something on Lucky?"

"There's no chance for him to escape. He beat this man to death with his hands; Harry Landrie is the dead man."

"Him!" grunted Bud. "Speaking personal, I'd give Lucky a medal for that."

The priest glanced sharply at him, started to speak, and then smoothed away the beginning of a smile. "Also," he said, "he abducted a girl—kidnapped a helpless girl, Bud."

"That changes it! Well, I guess Jud Nevil will make

103

things warm for Lucky. Let's go around and see the sheriff.''

"He'll be pretty busy, Bud.''

"That's all right. He's always got a place in his office for friends of mine. I'll introduce you, Father Connell.''

They started around the barn and into the main street.

"Between you and me,'' said Bud, "I ain't sorry this has happened.''

The priest shook his head.

"No matter what the crimes of Lucky Bill, I am not glad to see any man outlawed, Bud.''

"He's got it coming, but what tickles me is that the sheriff will have to use me this time.''

"And how's that?''

"Always before when they was a manhunt, he'd say that he didn't need no special help, but when it comes to Lucky Bill he'll have to admit that he needs every man that can pull a gun. Here we are, Father.''

It was not often that there was such a bustle around the office of Sheriff Nevil. During his early days in office, Wheeler had been notoriously a storm center; but Jud Nevil had discouraged the lawless. A bull-terrier joy in fighting for the sake of the fight, an endless patience on the trail, and no mean ability with weapons—with such an equipment Nevil had made Wheeler an uneasy resort for those not on speaking terms with the law. And as a result he was often pining in idleness during this term in his office. For even the most daredevil among the lawless were not eager to enter his territory; there were easier hunting grounds nearby.

This day, however, there was joyous activity around the little building which consisted of the sheriff's office, his living quarters, and the jail, all in different wings, and altogether by no means a large house. Bud led the way into the outer office where two deputies were busy at paper work; but neither of them quite so busy as he wished to appear.

"Any news, my friends?" asked the priest.

He was met by a curt nope from one of the men, who immediately ran on to add that the sheriff was sending out a "flock of telegrams;" that Lucky Bill would be an outlaw by order of the state government in a few moments, perhaps, and that even then they were preparing preliminary notices in pen and ink, to be set up here and there and fill the interval until the printed warnings against Lucky Bill could be struck off.

All these details were grunted out amidst a profuse rustling of papers, and in the end there was an announcement that they were far too busy to talk. The good priest might have taken this for final and turned away—for he had learned all he hoped to know. But his sleeve was pulled by Bud, who shook his head solemnly.

"That's only Kurt Janver," he whispered. "He don't know nothing. Wait a minute. Hey, Kurt," he added aloud, "let's see the sheriff, will you?"

"Sheriff's busy," announced Kurt absently. He jerked up his head. "Run along, kid. Got no time for you today."

"You'd think," said the boy with irritating calm, to Father Connell, "that these gents never had any business before. But Janver, there, is a new hand. He gets rattled dead easy."

Kurt Janver flushed furiously. "Did the sheriff tell you that?" he asked.

"Him? What he tells me ain't the only things I know. You've picked up that same paper four times and put it

105

down again. What's the matter, Kurt?''

"One of these days—" Kurt began darkly and left the sentence unfinished. "Slope, Bud! The sheriff wants things quiet.''

"You ain't keeping your voice down, none. There he comes now.''

For the door to the inner office opened, and the little sheriff appeared at the threshold. He had one of those lean, lined faces which ever have an expression of melancholy and which gave a deceptive suggestion of frailty to his body. His hair was just sufficient to be transparent and make his baldness more striking. And that baldness lifted his forehead to an intellectual height. Except for his sun-browned skin the sheriff looked more of a clerk than a man of action.

"What's all this noise?" he asked in his quiet way. "What did I tell you, Kurt?"

"It's the kid," said Janver sullenly. "You got him raised up like a pet, and he keeps bothering."

The sheriff frowned and parted his lips to speak sternly to Bud; but the latter raised his hand and broke in hastily:

"That's all right, Sheriff. Don't be hard on Kurt. I don't mind a bit what he says.''

The sheriff's wrath was checked. He set his teeth and kept back a smile.

"Besides," went on Bud, "they wasn't any way Kurt could figure why you'd want me about now."

"And why should I be wanting you right about now, son?"

"Ain't you got Lucky Bill on your hands?"

At this remark the sheriff chuckled.

"Right!" he said. "Maybe I'll be needing you, son.

But just now I'm talking strict business."

"Just my line," said the irrepressible Bud. "I ain't no girl to chatter about nothing when they's work on hand. By the way, meet my friends, Father Connell."

The sheriff became grave as he extended his hand.

"I've heard of you, Father," he said; "besides, you come well introduced."

Neither of them dared to smile, for the eye of Bud was upon them.

"Mr. Aiken is inside," went on the sheriff. "He's told me that you know his daughter better than any one, and perhaps you could give us some practical advice. Her recovery is our big job, of course. Lucky Bill comes second with me."

"Hark at him talk," chuckled Bud. "He'd sell a crown for a crack at Lucky. I've heard him say so."

"Come in, then, Father Connell," said the sheriff, favoring Bud with a scowl, "and we'll talk things over."

But Bud was upon their heels as they went toward the door. He said to the priest: "I told you I'd get you in."

"But what about you?" growled Sheriff Nevil.

"Why," cried Bud, "you ain't going to tackle Bill without me, are you?"

A roar of laughter went up from every one in the room, and Bud became a dark crimson. Under cover of that noise the priest said: "Why not, Sheriff?"

"No reason why not. Come in, Bud, and don't talk till you're spoke to."

They filed into the door, Bud favoring Kurt Janver with a grimace of mockery. Inside they found Henry Aiken pacing excitedly up and down; he greeted Father Connell with the words: "We got him, Father. The sheriff is wiring the capital of the state. We'll have him outlawed in a minute or so—the boys can hunt him the way they'd hunt a coyote—for his scalp. But who's this?''

He scowled at Bud, and the latter met his eye unabashed.

"Don't mind me," asserted Bud. "Don't pay no attention to me till you get in a pinch. Then I'll pitch in and help."

"What's the meaning of this, Sheriff?" asked the rancher angrily.

"An old head," said the sheriff with meaning, "and a tongue that don't wag. He'll be all right here, Mr. Aiken. Once more, you promise to keep control of your temper when Mat Morgan comes?"

"Damn him—yes. As long as I don't have to talk to him. But he's the cause of all this."

"He's coming down the street now with his arm tied up. Now, Mr. Aiken, get hold of yourself. Make Mat mad and we'll have him against us; treat him smooth and he'll maybe be with us."

"What'll bring him on our side?"

"Because he'll want to see Lucky caught. I know these gunfighters like a book, Aiken. Lucky beat him fair and square in public; he'll never rest till he's either beat Lucky or else got Lucky filled full of lead by somebody else. Steady, now. Here he comes. If you can't smile at him, Aiken, don't meet his eye."

And at that moment a knock came on the door; it was opened to Mat Morgan himself. His jaunty bearing alone was a sufficient proof of the slightness of his wound; it had nipped through the flesh only, without tearing, and except for the uselessness of that arm, Mat Morgan was unchanged.

The moment his eyes fell on the group in the room, he halted, and with a deft movement of his heel he blocked the retrograde movement of the door and dropped his sound hand to his hip. He was a real two-gun man, and still a fighting force in spite of his wound.

"What's the reception committee for, Nevil?" he asked.

The sheriff answered blandly: "All gents that know something we want to learn. You know Mr. Aiken. Here's Father Connell. And this is Bud; you don't mind him?"

"A bright kid is like a bright hoss—I don't trust 'em an inch," said Mat Morgan coldly, eyeing the boy. "But let him stay. I got nothing to say I want kept dark. My story is short and quick. Molly Aiken was hounded sick by him that's dead—I mean Landrie. She wrote me and asked me to slide down there and take her away."

"A bare-faced lie!" roared Aiken. "If they was any truth in it, I'd disown the girl."

The sheriff sprang up in some alarm. "Steady, Mat!" he called. "Don't mind him. Mr. Aiken, another break like that and you leave the office."

"Another break like that," said Mat coldly, "and he'll have to be carried out. I'm talking fact. I was on my way after her when I had the smash with Lucky Bill. My gun hung—it gave him an advantage—and he gave me this for a keepsake." The face of Mat whitened with venomous emotion.

"Then he tied me up and pretended to get real friendly. I didn't mind. It was his luck that had beat me, not him. We got to talking. I told him about my trip being spoiled. Then he said he'd go and get the girl for me."

"You let him?" asked the sheriff.

"Me?" growled Mat. "You think I'm a cross between a fool and a skunk? Trust Molly to him? I told him he was crazy. But he said he'd go anyway and keep the appointment for me. I knew what that meant. So I figured a way to beat him, pretended to fall in with his scheme, and told him the longest way round to the ranch. Then I got Harry Landrie and told him what had happened, and told him to cut through the hills and get to the house in time to warn the girl's folks, but—"

"You sent Harry Landrie on a message like that?" sneered Aiken.

"I done just that. A gent like you can't understand, but it's a fact. Landrie was my rival; but I'd rather of seen Molly married to him than seen her carried off the way she's been by a no-good skunk!"

Even Aiken had nothing to say. It was a crushing victory for Mat Morgan, and he turned pale with a sense of his own self-sacrificing virtue. Father Connell was moved to a smile of infinite tenderness, and the sheriff frowned in bewilderment.

"That's the whole story," said Mat Morgan. "But Landrie's hoss must of gone lame, and he got there late—they say you found his hoss lame in the hills. And Lucky got Molly; and I'll get him for doing it! It's the second thing between us!"

"My heavens, man!" groaned Aiken, throwing out his arms. "Did you tell it to only one man? You should have raised the town!"

"Raised the town?" sneered Mat Morgan, "and told 'em that Molly Aiken was ready to leave home with the first gent that come along?"

Again he had scored a point heavily. Aiken had nothing to say.

He could only murmur after a moment: "But where does this lead us to, Sheriff? Where's all the valuable information we was going to get out of Mat Morgan?"

The sheriff shook his head, puzzled. "I thought they'd be more to Mat's yarn," he said. "It don't look like it leads us anywhere, and that's a fact."

"Sheriff," piped Bud, "can I speak?"

"They ain't anybody else making a sensible noise," said the sheriff gloomily. "What's in your head, Bud?"

"When Lucky left, where'd he tell Mat that he'd bring the girl?"

"Out to my shack on the West Road," said Mat. "What of it?"

"Ain't there a chance that he'll do what he promised? Ain't there a chance that he ain't a skunk?" asked Bud.

There was a general shaking of heads; but an idea came to Mat Morgan.

"Gents," he said, "we got one hope. Maybe Lucky will ride in just to crow over me and tell me he's got the girl cached away. It ain't much of a chance, but it's the only one they is. When he comes—if he does—you could have some of the boys in the willows, all handy, Sheriff."

It was so thin a hope that the suggestion was received without enthusiasm, yet it was decided without more ado to act upon it. Mat Morgan was to return to his shack on the West Road; the sheriff and some picked men were to be hidden in the willows; and they would wait for the coming of Lucky Bill that day or the next. The bustle of preparation began, and Bud managed to corner the sheriff for an instant.

"I guess this is my chance, Sheriff?" he asked eagerly. "I got my old gat all oiled up and ready. You'll let me come along?"

His voice was made deep and manly for the occasion, but his eyes were misty with eagerness. The sheriff shook his head.

"I tell you how it is, son; if Lucky was to see you when he was hurrying by he might take you for a man and turn loose a man-sized slug at you. I wouldn't have that on my mind for the rest of my life for ten times the reward. Bud, you stay home till you're a pile bigger'n you are now. Now leave me go; I'm some rushed!"

"Sheriff," asked Bud bitterly, "who brung up the idea of where to lay for Lucky?"

"Why, in a way, you did, son; and when we split the reward I'll see you get a share."

"Damn the reward!" exclaimed Bud. "I want the chance at the fight. For the last time, partner, I ask you man to man: Do I get the chance?"

At any other time the sheriff would probably have noted the use of that word "partner," which was passing the lips of Bud for the first time in his life; he would have understood, also, the vital quality of that appeal.

But he was hurried, and his mind was fixed on the work which might lie ahead of him. It would be the greatest day in his life if he should run down Lucky Bill as an outlaw, and his heartbeat quickened at the thought.

"Bud," he said, "you ain't in your place. Stay home. I'll tell you why later."

Without another word, Bud stood aside. But he remained motionless, looking rather sadly after the hurrying form of the sheriff.

"Only a minute ago," he said, "I would of called

him my best friend." He winked the tears out of his eyes and swallowed hard. "These here things s what makes a man," he said grimly. "Besides, can't I play a lone hand?"

Chapter Eleven

The Past

For each of the three steps that Lucky made into the sanctum of Jefferson Taliaferro, he discovered a new set of wonders. First, he was aware of bookcases higher than his head that ran around the big library; next he saw a range of painted men and women framed above the books; and last, coming well inside the apartment, a swarm of details rushed on his eyes.

Leaded glass windows, with dark-red velvet curtains draped beside them; a red thick carpet underfoot; a mighty fireplace equipped with brass andirons, iron crane, and great copper kettle; from the center of the ceiling a big copper lamp hanging from chains poised above with a counter weight; wrought iron candlesticks in the corners of the room; two ships' models of imposing size and delicate craftsmanship; a cabinet of curios;

another filled with more styles of weapons than even Lucky had ever dreamed of; a colorful globe ready to turn on its standard; Windsor chairs, wing chairs in profusion; a lengthy table, in itself an architectural piece, and strewed with papers; all of these things swept upon the bewildered eyes and brain of Lucky Bill so that he was more disarmed than if a loaded gun had been held to his head, and he was not even aware of the delight of his host, standing at one side to enjoy the confusion of his guest.

Here, then, was the retreat in which the hermit truly lived. The rest of his mansion became a hopeless ruin. He was content with this while the last years of his life withered away. But in spite of this, the character of the rest of the house had invaded the room. There was an air of crumbling splendor about this place which was even more suggestive of death and decay than the other dusty apartments in the house. The threadbare weight of the velvet curtains seemed about to tear them from their fastenings above. It was enough to make one hold one's breath to imagine such a fall, and the thin, choking, age-old cloud of dust that they would cast up in their fall.

The ships' models, too, had gone from white wood to yellow to an orange-black-brown, and one blow on them might reduce the whole to a ruin. The black logs smoldering on the hearth seemed to give no more than a painted heat; the wood smoke that drifted through the wood faintly was stale to the nostrils; the papers littering the huge table seemed yellow-edged; the book lying opened face downward was crushed flat as though it had lain in exactly that position for some half century.

In a word, there was no life in that great room. For all its crowd of objects it was empty. The soul was gone.

As if, on a day long past, a vigorous man had come in his reading to the mention of a far land, had tossed the book upon the table, had strode to that globe and turned it to the place that was named, had rushed out of the house, and departed for the far goal never to return. And in his place there remained this white-headed wisp of mortality, Jefferson Taliaferro! And this man was also a ruin. Only his voice was young and mocked himself, his house, and all his possessions.

The little old fellow returned from closing the door. He rubbed his hands and blew out his breath after the manner of one who has come in out of an icy night; and indeed the rest of that big house had the effect of cold. Coming to the fireplace, he raised the tongs with arms that trembled with the weight, and hauled one fire-rotted log on top of two more.

From the side of the hearth he took the great old bellows, the leather turned by age to a beautiful and rich brown. Under the blast from this implement the fire whizzed into a white spot, a blue, stiff-standing flame; and when he stopped his ministrations the good yellow light went tossing high up the chimney.

It redeemed a semicircle out of the gloom of the apartment, and the cheery region embraced a deep-seated Windsor and the mighty wing chair which Lucky could see at a glance was the habitual throne of old Taliaferro.

But the old man was not yet ready to sit down. He went first to a cupboard at the side of the room, and from this brought out a tall-necked bottle, green as emerald, and a pair of slender-stemmed glasses. He poured for them each a brimming glass of white wine—rather, it was of a delicate golden tinge that sparkled amazingly in the firelight and took on, at the borders of the glass, many changing tones of color. Lucky held the drink in his hand and grinned over the brim of the glass at his host.

"What I can't make out," he confided to Jefferson Taliaferro, "is whether this is made to look at or to drink."

The other raised his busy white brows, but gradually decided not to take offense. "In the language of this region," he said in his definite way, "it is decidedly *not* what is called a drink. The alcoholic content is small. It stirs the imagination, not the blood. Sir, I drink your health and your happiness."

Lucky met the gesture with a similar one, and tasted his drink. It was truly a delicate flavor. And a strange one to a tongue which had been so often scorched by the fiery red-eye, and stung by the sandy winds of the desert. And the fragrance, literally, clung to his palate like an air blowing over wide fields of wild flowers. It was an enchanting drink to Lucky Bill. Over the brim of his lowered glass he stared again at Taliaferro, and this time with a new understanding; he came to know, at a step, just why the old fellow was smiling and nodding so cheerily above the wine.

"Mr. Taliaferro," he declared solemnly, "this here liquor—which it ain't got the taste of liquor, nor the sting—this here liquor is drink and music and perfume all rolled up together."

Old Taliaferro surveyed him with a slit of twinkling eyes. "On the whole," he said, "I don't know that it's ever been more aptly described. My cellar grows low, but while it lasts I live. Here is the house that I built with my will and my hands—" He made a gesture above him.

Looking to the massive paneling of the ceiling far above them, Lucky could scarcely forbear a headshake of wonder. That withered memory of a man had done all this?

"Here is the house," went on Jefferson Taliaferro. "It is growing old. It comes to an end, slowly, just as my cellar and as I myself are doing. Yet it still stands. No one but myself knows how near the cellar is to the end; nor how far the rot has eaten away the good heart's-wood of the stanchions and beams that support this house—"

Here Lucky started; he would not have been surprised if at that moment he had heard a rending and grinding of breaking wood above him, and seen the ceiling bulge down and splinter across.

The antiquarian continued: "But the last bottle of wine is as good as the first; and the house, I trust, still looks strong enough from a distance, sir?"

"Aye, strong enough," muttered Lucky uneasily.

"And therefore my hope is not altogether without foundation—that my cellar and my house and I shall all hold out together until the last day, and at the last day collapse into nothingness."

"Friend," said Lucky, "that wine sure has a queer kick. Here it's made you start hanging crape all over a pretty snug little party. Cheer up, Mr. Taliaferro."

"Cheer up? Why, sir, I was never in better spirits. I wish to go down with my house like a captain with his ship. Is there anything sad in that? No! My only fear is to pass away as the millions pass away—unheeded—unnoted—unmourned. My sorrow is the thought of strangers breaking down my doors, walking through my halls, and coming into this very room, sir, when this room is empty of me."

A palsy shook his hand. He leaned his head against the chair and closed his eyes until his composure returned

"Look you, my young friend, there is a duty that depends on a man who is the last of his line. A grave and a great duty. He must bring it to an end fittingly. The great sentence may have been written by others, but if he can only put a distinctive period at the end of it, one portion of all the glory of the others of his blood comes upon him. And I am the last of the line. You see what it means?"

In his interest he rose, sprang up like a youth in enthusiasm, and caught out from its holder a thick-bodied candle. With Lucky trailing him, a huge form behind the little man, Jefferson Taliaferro approached the wall, holding the candle high above his head until the radiance struck one of the paintings full in the face.

It was a dim work. The paint was cracked, blackened, even peeling away, it seemed. But Lucky made out the outlines of a stern and bearded face, a morion upon his head, and a cuirass about his body, and the hilt of the sword at his side.

"There's Roger Taliaferro, the first of the line to come to this country. Aye, there were others before him, but when the Revolution came we disclaimed the older line. We began new—free souls—a free country—a clean air. We date ourselves from Roger. We? I am all that is left! Well, he began it. And here's his wife, Anne Taliaferro. She was a Mordaunt. Anne Taliaferro When I was a lad I used to stand and wonder at this face and swear I'd never marry till I met the girl as fair in the face and as clean in the eye as Anne Taliaferro—and that's why I'm a bachelor to this day, by heaven!

"Do you wonder at it? Look at the sweep of those white arms, and see how she turns her head, so proudly and so mildly, and mark her smile! Tush—a smile like that is worth more than gold! It makes a whole race of men rich with the bare memory of it."

Perhaps the excitement had struck to the old fellow's mind; or perhaps he was seeing with the eye of his youth when the picture was still clear. But now it was even more sadly faded than the portrait of her husband. Yet Lucky Bill seemed to see the very smile of which his companion spoke. He, too, became strangely excited; he had raised his head high and a faint and proud smile was at the corners of his mouth. He went with a soft step behind Jefferson Taliaferro.

"Here's Hubert. He sailed the Spanish Main, stanch old Hubert, and laid his ship between two of the pirate's, Mortimer's, and sank 'em both. Afterward they say he sailed a bit on the shady side of the law himself. But he never stole from the poor, and he never gave to the rich, and there's the true spirit of the Taliaferros. Mark you John now, a Puritanical fellow, but he had his history—and a long one and a bold one. There was more behind that smug smile than you'd guess.

"Now Sylvester, with a face as dainty as a lady's. He went to London and ruffled it with the blades yonder, and stained his own point more than once, says the legend. Now Francis, who fought from seventy-five to eighty-three, and got his ten wounds and an empty purse for his pains.

"Bartholomew sailed under Captain Hull. Hush! I can hear his big bull voice and the songs he used to sing when I was a wee lad. Then Peter—he was a vain man, was Peter. And Roderick, my father, who fought in Texas, for Texas, and died to free her. God bless him! He pulled down more than one when he fell. And so the tale ends."

He lowered the candle; but though his hand shook, his eye was bright.

"That brings the story down to me, and my rotted house. Do you know why I tell you all this, lad? Because you told me how William Taliaferro died—like a man. He and his son, they ended the other side of the line. And tonight for the first time I envy our black sheep, William. He died a man's death, you say, in the rocks, with his gun in his hand—perjuring his soul, no doubt, but swearing his innocence like a true Taliaferro for the sake of the fair name of his race. But, ah, lad! What manner of death can come to a man like me to do honor to my line?"

So saying, his hand fell so abruptly that the flame of the candle snapped out, and they were left in a grimly changed light. During the last few minutes the dawn had been increasing rapidly, and now that the candle was out Jefferson Taliaferro stood in the light of the new day, which was falling coldly through the leaded panes of the window beside him.

For the first time in his life Lucky Bill thought of death, and he was afraid.

Chapter Twelve

A Woman's Way

It was nearly noon before Molly Aiken came down to them. They had left the house and walked through the wrecked environs of the place—among the rotten sheds and the tumbled barns which had once been mighty buildings.

A close feeling seemed to have grown up in the breast of the old man for his companion. He referred to it once or twice in actual words—more often Lucky was made to feel it by inference, as though he, Lucky, was the only man in the world who could come so close to the heart of Jefferson Taliaferro. And the reason was that he had been the bearer of good tidings—he had brought a story which restored to Jefferson good faith, pride in the memory of that other Taliaferro who had died in the arms of Lucky.

"Why," said he, "I feel that you are almost a relation, Lucky. You have had the blood of our family on your clothes—on your hands, eh?"

The very name seemed to please Jefferson Taliaferro. Sometimes in a pause of the conversation he would begin to repeat softly, "Lucky! Lucky!" and then he would look askance at his companion and laugh with childish delight.

It was in the midst of one of these controlled bursts of mirth that another sound struck down at them from the upper part of the house—for they had come back into it and were sitting in the big library. It was the singing of Molly Aiken as she came down the stairs, running; it brought Jefferson Taliaferro out of his chair with a gasp, and he stood in a stiff posture—partly erect, partly stooped toward the chair. His eyes were the eyes of one who sees a ghost.

"The girl!" he exclaimed suddenly, as one painfully relieved. "I forgot her. For a moment I thought—"

Whatever his thought was, he brushed it away by passing his hand across his eyes; and he and Lucky went to meet her. It was the first time that the latter had seen her in the daylight, and he started at the change in her. The moon had whitened her, made her more statuesque, more reserved, and there had been about her a harmonious air of melancholy romance—the girl, helpless, fleeing from her family to her lover.

Keen daylight brushed these illusions away. She was not lovely in the true sense of the word, but she was charmingly pretty. So far from being a crystal white, her skin was richly colored olive—the clear olive of the outdoors. More than beauty of features her charm was her manner, her inexhaustible spirit. There was something about her walk that expressed a keen delight in living; and in an hour of talk her face was never twice the same, but passed through an infinity of moods.

As she ran down the last of the stairs and came across the dusty old hall toward them Lucky had a different thought for every step she took, until when she paused before them she had stepped into her new character, in his eyes, and he had adjusted himself to her. She greeted them, and in the second word had found something to laugh about with Jefferson Taliaferro, and when he heard her Lucky remembered at length that the object of all this labor was to take her to Mat Morgan.

The thought dropped on his spirit like a burden on the shoulders, and kept him gloomily silent during her breakfast. Yet that was quite a gala occasion. They went into the kitchen, to the dismay of George, who was struggling to provide his finest meal for that morning, and everything was topsy-turvy for a long time.

But the misery of Lucky increased. Not that he felt himself to be in love; he only knew that every time she smiled he damned Mat Morgan. If she became pensive for a moment he damned Mat Morgan nevertheless, for he attributed her thought to that gay battler.

She noted his gloom at length and rallied him for it, but he returned no answer. Finally he rose sullenly from the table.

"We're overdue at the end of our trip," he said. "I'll go out and saddle up." And with that he left them.

Had he known what went on when he left the room he would have played eavesdropper shamelessly, for the door had no sooner closed behind him than the girl dropped her hands hopelessly into her lap and stared in actual terror at her host.

"Stop him!" she cried faintly. "Stop him, Mr. Tali-aferro! I won't go!"

The old man was naturally too bewildered to answer. Instead he rose and went toward the door, but she checked him again.

"Not that! Don't call to him!"

"My dear Miss Aiken, why not?"

"Because that will bring him back. He mustn't know!"

"Know what?"

"Why I won't go on."

At this he returned to the table, and with a glance sent old George scurrying out of the kitchen. "Now, my dear, what is wrong? Where are you going and why won't you go there? And why won't you tell Lucky?"

"It's too long a story—and he's saddling!"

"I don't want your story. I don't want to pry into your affairs. But tell me enough so that I can help you."

"Ah," breathed Molly Aiken, "I've been a selfish coward; I don't dare tell you! Besides, you couldn't help me."

"Perhaps you underestimate me," said the old fellow soberly, and a spot of red came in his cheeks. "I assure you of this: that if you give me a good reason for stopping Lucky, he shall not take you a step out of this house."

"Mr. Taliaferro, the last man who tried to stop him is dead." She caught her breath. "You won't use that against him?"

At this juxtaposition of contradictions he threw up his hands; but when they were lowered again he was smiling at her.

"I shall tell you this much to let you know my exact

125

position: I have never met in my memory a boy to whom I am drawn so much. Certainly I shall use nothing you say against him. But in one breath you accuse him; in the next breath you say you fear to harm him? What does it mean?''

"I have not accused him. Not a syllable of accusation. But I cannot go on."

"Madame, my brain begins to spin."

"Have I time to tell you?"

"We shall make time. George, George! Bolt the doors—let no one in! We are accustomed to securing the house. Now—"

"Bolts won't keep him out if he wants to come in."

"Lady," said the old man, bowing profoundly to her, "you have remarkable confidence in him; before you leave I shall hope to give you an equal confidence in me. Besides, he will not have the horse ready for some moments, and you are wasting time."

"I tell you all in one word, though you won't understand. Mr. Taliaferro, I have committed a crime—I have been headstrong, willful. My father and I quarreled about a man he wished me to marry. I was stubborn; he was furious; I wrote to another man and asked him to come and take me away."

"A man you loved?"

She winced.

"I was so angry at father that I thought I loved him. It was anything to get away. It was Mat Morgan; but on his way he had a quarrel with Lucky and was shot—slightly wounded. Then Lucky found out what he had done and came in place of Mat to bring me up to Mat's house. He found me waiting. I'd gone to the place where I told Mat I would be, and I was waiting there to tell him when he came that I'd changed my mind. That I couldn't go; that I was sick with shame—that I didn't love him enough for that, and I preferred to go back and face Dad. But when Lucky came he thought my unwillingness was simply a sign that I feared him—didn't trust him to be Mat's true messenger. And because he'd promised Mat he made me come with him—forced me!"

"Ah!" murmured Jefferson Taliaferro, and he rocked a little from side to side. One would have thought that the old man was listening to delightful music.

"I went. There was nothing I could have done—he would have gagged and bound me and carried me on his horse otherwise. I made one attempt to give the alarm—cried out once—and then he stopped my mouth with his hand. I promised to go on and make no more outcries, but that one call had been heard.

"From the sounds at the ranch house I knew my father was taking out his cowpunchers to follow me. In the meantime we went on. We were stopped on the way by the man my father wanted me to marry. He wouldn't fight Lucky with his revolver, but he fought him with his fists. It was a terrible fight—"

"Lucky's face is cut—ah!"

"And Harry fought foul, but in the end Lucky knocked him down. His head struck a rock—he died. Then we went on. My father caught sight of me and followed—came close enough to recognize Lucky, I'm afraid—and though we finally got away, I know he's on the trail. And here we are, with a death on the head of Lucky—a death that will outlaw him. What can I do? I can't go on to Mat Morgan. I don't dare go back and face my father. Mr. Taliaferro, what can I do?"

The old man was looking past her, nodding, as though this were all a familiar tale to him.

"My dear," he said, "you trust me?"

"Yes—absolutely."

"Then stay with me here. I have no advice for you just now. But time is wiser than any man. Stay here and let time ripen. In the end this tangle will unravel itself. And I shall be happy to have you with me."

"Ah, if you could keep me, but listen!"

It was the voice of Lucky calling outside the house that the horses were ready.

"Keep him away!" moaned the girl.

"We'll bring him in here and explain everything just as you've explained it to me."

"No, no, no! Don't you know what kind of a man he is? He's promised Mat Morgan that he'll bring me to him. And nothing can keep him from it. Nothing!"

The knob of the door was turned, then it was shaken violently.

"Hello, what's this?" called Lucky.

Taliaferro stepped close. "Lucky," he said, "Miss Aiken has changed her mind. She's not riding with you."

A breathless silence answered him; it had a climatic quality to it, more than any words could have contained.

"I'm a reasonable man," said Lucky at length. "And I got a pretty fair eye for a joke, but this time I don't see where there's room for a joke. Tell Molly Aiken that I'm waiting for her."

"She knows that."

"And that if she don't come I'll bust open this door and get her!"

"Sir, are you in your senses?"

"I hope to tell a man I am, and I mean what I say."

"And do you know that if you break down that door against my will you are committing an act of burglary?"

"Damn the act of burglary!"

"And that as the owner of this house I have the right to defend my property from intruders—the right of shooting you down like a dog when you break the lock I have turned in that door?"

Again the deadly silence fell, and the old man and the girl stared at each other in the suspense. She was utterly colorless.

"Mr. Taliaferro," said a voice so hardened that it was unrecognizable, "either I'm dreaming all this or else you've gone crazy; but through this door I'm going to come."

"Then," said Taliaferro, "by my sacred word of honor, the moment you cross the threshold I shoot you down, and the law cannot lay a finger on me for it."

The girl rose from her chair with a gasp, but the old man turned to her and showed his empty hands.

"Taliaferro," continued Lucky with an ominous snarl in his voice, "I dunno that you've figured me right. But I'm a tolerable hard sort when I get going. I give you fair notice: I'm coming through that door!"

At the same instant, the words bitten off short by the shock, the door received a heavy impact—it split in the center from top to bottom and sagged in.

Another pause.

"I'm coming, shooting," said Lucky. "If you don't get me with the first slug you can lay a hundred to one that I'll drill you clean with the first shot. But before I come, I'm begging you to think it over. Taliaferro, you're an old man—I'd rather lose an arm than touch you. But I've give my word of honor, and the girl has got to go with me!''

To Molly Aiken, until this moment, it had all seemed a rather overdone farce! but now she saw Taliaferro step back to a corner of the room and lift from two pegs a double-barreled shotgun; and it suddenly came home to her that the whole thing was deadly earnest. For a moment both her voice and body were frozen; then she ran with a scream and threw herself close to the door as if she dreamed with her meager strength to bar the way to Lucky.

"Lucky," she pleaded hysterically, "it isn't Mr. Taliaferro alone who begs you to go. It's I as well. I can't go with you, Lucky; I can't go to Mat Morgan."

She heard him mutter: "It's a nightmare. I'll wake up in a minute back in the saloon at Wheeler with a bullet through my head and Mat Morgan standing over me. The whole thing has been a dream." He said aloud: "Molly, they ain't no woman in the world that I'd rather treat white; but I've give my word to Mat Morgan, and you got to come. Besides, I ask you, is this playing square and fair?"

"I thought I could go through with it," sobbed the girl, "but I can't."

He seemed to be staggered by this.

"Have you changed your mind about Mat?" he asked.

"I—yes," she said miserably.

"Molly," he said sternly, "they's one dead man on the way from you to Mat. Are you dead sure you've changed your mind about him?"

"Oh, Lucky," cried the girl, "I can't make you understand. Only try to forgive me and wait till I can explain.''

And finding that all words were nothing, she crumpled up at the base of the door and burst into tears. She expected the door to be burst into fragments, then to be caught up and borne away into the outer day.

But instead of that, after a moment the voice of Lucky said heavily: ''By right I'd ought to take you. I'd ought to come in and drop Taliaferro if he tries to stop me. Because both you and him have played crooked and you've done me wrong. But I can't do it—yet. I got to go to Mat and see how he stands, now that you've changed your mind about him. But if he says that he still wants you, and if he holds me to my promise, then write this down in red: I'll come after you to the end of the desert, and I'll bring you to him.''

That was all. His heels struck heavily across the quaking back porch. A moment later a horse snorted under the spur and galloping hoofbeats thudded off into the distance.

Chapter Thirteen

The Snare

Suppose Napoleon on the eve of Montenotte, recalled by the directors, and a rival commander given the execution of the combinations which he had planned, the grief and fury of the little Corsican would have been nothing as compared with the disappointment of Bud when the sheriff calmly dropped him out of the scheme which had originated, in the germ, in the head of Bud himself.

Bud had long felt himself a man; he had proved it to his own satisfaction by soundly thrashing, at one time or another, every boy in Wheeler. And when one is greater than a boy, what is he if not a man? All that remained was to demonstrate his maturity to the older male population of the village, and in the pursuit of Lucky Bill, Bud had seen a golden opportunity.

The full realization of the blow came to him only gradually. He stood about in a daze after the sheriff had definitely announced that he wanted nothing in short pants in his posse; in a daze he heard the elaboration of the plans. The sheriff would cache his men near the shack of Mat Morgan. If, as was barely possible, Lucky brought the girl with him to Mat in fulfillment of his promise, then all would be well-at one blow Lucky would be shot down and the girl retaken.

Or, if Lucky came alone, which was more probable, then he would be permitted to go into Mat's shack unhindered. While there Mat would try to draw from him the whereabouts of the girl. As soon as he had definitely failed or succeeded, he would give a signal to the sheriff's men.

If it were dark he would move a lamp to a window. If it were day he would close the shutter of the same window. And then the posse would rush the shack and take Lucky or kill him—it mattered not which. Mat Morgan had already been sent on ahead in a buckboard, for with his wound it was painful for him to ride in a saddle.

All of this the boy heard agreed upon, and yet it seemed impossible that the sheriff would leave with his men without taking him—Bud—the wellspring of the whole plan. Yet the preparations for departure sped along, and no one noticed him. No invitation was cast his way.

They could not know that they were heaping dry ashes upon his heart when they slapped him on the shoulder in passing and called him a "bright kid."

"Kid!" The very word was an abomination to him. Now and then he caught the quiet eye of Father Connell upon him and he avoided the glance of the priest. The sheriff paused near him on a hurried errand.

"You can lay to this, Bud: I'll see that you get your full share of the reward if anything comes out of this. You make the tenth—here's the draft of the bulletin that'll be out about Lucky as soon as we can get it printed. Take it and figure out for yourself what your share will be. Look here—two thousand from the state. Besides that, three thousand that Aiken is putting up. That makes a cold five thousand, and your share would be five hundred."

He chuckled.

"Why, what'd you do with that much money, son?"

"Son!" Another word loathed by Bud. He looked at the sheriff with a dull eye.

"Damn the money!" he said quietly. "I want the fun!"

It sent Nevil into a peal of laughter. He repeated the remark to the seven chosen men who were to ride with him; and they raised another chorus of mirth. There were good-humored jests; Bud was told again that he was a nervy "*kid*," and a game "shaver." And every word made him writhe.

Yet he could not realize the full extent of his rebuff until the party was mounted. Their last look and the last word was for him; they waved their hands to him and swore that they would bring back his money to him safe and in full; and then they were gone with a rush. In a moment the cloud of dust bulged up from the street and they dissolved in its midst. And then the heart of Bud became utterly empty.

He looked vacantly down at the poster. It was one of a score or so that the sheriff had had drawn up on tough linen-backed paper to be nailed up in prominent places in Wheeler and adjoining villages until the printed forms could be obtained and distributed.

There was no picture; indeed, there was none to be had. The poster set forth, in brief, that a reward of 2,000 dollars was offered for the apprehension of the man known as Lucky Bill—full name unknown—dead or alive. Hair, yellow.

Bud called into his mind the color of the hair which adorned the head of Bessie Williams—a glassy straw shade. Eyes, blue. Height, six feet and one or two inches. Weight, about 190.

"Easy—dead easy to put a bullet into a gent as big as that," decided Bud.

He reverted to the more particular description and strove to visualize it. Nose, straight or slightly aquiline. Lean face. Square jaw.

"What's aquiline mean?" muttered Bud aloud.

An answer came unexpectedly to him.

"Aquiline means curved, like the beak of an eagle, Bud." It was the priest, and Bud wondered at him. Then he flushed.

"How long have I been talking aloud?" he asked angrily, and half ashamed.

"First thing you've said."

Father Connell came closer.

"Bud," he said, "I think I understand. It's hard for you, but when you're a little older—"

It was the crowning blow to Bud. To be treated lightly by such a man as the sheriff—one whom he had felt to be his friend—was bad enough; to be pitied by a sky pilot was too much for the heart of the boy to endure.

For a moment he stared at the priest with a face convulsed. Then, since a queer tightening of the muscles of his throat warned him of the approach of a shameful catastrophe, he whirled on his heel and fled.

Down the street, behind the Alcazar Saloon, and fast as a darting swallow to the little shed where Buck Chapman allowed Bud to keep his horse. Through the door he raced. The white-faced Pinto whirled at him, with ears flattened, but recognized his master in time to raise one whimsical ear again.

Then the arms of Bud were flung around his neck, the face of Bud was pressed against the tangles of the mane, and queer sounds began to rise from the middle of the boy's body and break in moans at his lips.

It was the first time he had wept since his very childhood. His hard fortune had skilled him in controlling all show of emotion, and now this noisy agony frightened him. He did not understand it. But it seemed to Bud that his heart was being torn in two, and that those convulsive sobs relieved the pain.

The fear conquered the weeping at length. Finally he choked down the sobs and whirled toward the door. There was no one there. He ran to it and closed it and stood with his shoulder pressed against it. He was numb with fear. He could not move, although Pinto followed him in wonder and tipped the sombrero from his head with an inquisitive nose.

He knew now. He had been crying like a girl who had stubbed her toe—or been spanked. He had been crying. He, Bud, who aspired to manhood!

The terrible shame made him numb and sick. He was almost afraid to meet the keen eye of Pinto, lest he had understood. But what if he had been seen? What if someone had stolen up behind him and seen him sobbing with his arms around the neck of the horse? What if even now a murmur were going up and down the street of Wheeler? What if, when he appeared, they should snicker behind his back and point after him? Hitherto he had been beyond their reach. But with ridicule they could make him weak, helpless. After a time, he ventured to open the door to the shed and look out. There was nothing living in sight except the Tompkins black cat, which was rolling in the sun and striking foolishly at the air. It reassured him to see this empty row of backyards; he went back to Pinto.

Of all the world it was plain that only Pinto understood his full value. As for the children of the village, they both feared and hated him. But their esteem mattered not a jot to Bud. Only the men counted, and the men had hopelessly estranged him that day. One by one he called up their faces, heard their patronizing voices. Chiefly, his rage centered on the sheriff, the false friend, and an overwhelming desire rose in him to prove his value to the men of Wheeler—to establish his manhood by one great stroke.

His hand touched the poster, crumpled in his pocket, and he drew it out again.

Two thousand dollars, and three thousand dollars from Mr. Aiken. Suppose one man were to take Lucky Bill single-handed? All that fortune would be his, undivided. Before Bud a bright succession of pictures unrolled—guns, saddles, horses, fine boots, spurs—his imagination halted before the prospect. He heard, like a murmuring organ music, the distant whispers of admiration which would surround him when he rode forth in his splendor—the captor of Lucky Bill!

Tears of joy rose in Bud's eyes, and at that moment

137

he made up his mind irrevocably. Under his vest he fumbled at the old revolver, slung from around his neck and worn out of sight because he would have been jeered had the children seen him carrying such a man's weapon. Then he looked to Pinto. When the little mustang was rounded up the year before and ridden, a cruel-minded jester had put a bur under the saddle of the bronco buster, and Pinto had gone mad with pain and fear.

He connected the pain with the saddle and not with the rider, and had bucked to get rid of the former, not the latter. The result was that he pitched four successive riders on that historic day, and won a glowing repute as an outlaw. Then he was taken as a show horse, and wherever there was a bucking bee, Pinto was brought to try out the prowess of the best riders.

In the end his education as a "bad hoss" was a polished thing. His article of pitching was a thing at which sage cowpunchers nodded in reverence; and Pinto was never ridden until long months of no care and much abuse reduced him to a shambling, red-eyed devil, and in this wise he was brought to Wheeler. He was done up—useless. And they turned him loose.

When he broke into Chapman's shed, Bud found him there and entered into diplomatic relations with the wild mustang. Crushed barley did what force had never done, enabled a human hand to steal up and touch Pinto between the eyes. And that was the beginning of a deep friendship. He would never bear even the sight of a saddle; but he was quite willing to have a blanket and thin strip of leather cinched around him, and after that he would go along readily with a thump of Bud's bare heels to impel him instead of the rip and prick of a pair of spurs. He hated bits, but Bud was entirely content with a piece of rope slung around his neck and over his nose, and Pinto obeyed the pull on that rope as if it had been a Mexican curb.

Chapman allowed Bud to keep the horse or in the shed, and when flesh returned to the outlaw he rounded into shape as a slim-bodied, deep-chested, iron-muscled beauty. And he was entirely Bud's own.

Once Chapman tried to ride him; afterward he was in bed for a month, and from that date no one questioned Bud's sole right to the horse.

This was the comrade, then, who was to go forth on the quest of adventure with Bud. The preparations were quickly made. Ten minutes after Bud made up his mind, he had cinched the blanket on Pinto, made up a knapsack of provisions, settled his ragged old sombrero over his eyes, thrust his bare toes into the rope loops which served him as stirrups, and was cantering swiftly away from Wheeler and into the mountain desert beyond. Lucky Bill was his goal.

2402
2407

Chapter Fourteen

The Big Man

He had no definitely settled plan. Vaguely he felt that the infallible sheriff must be right, and that his net would capture Lucky in the cabin of Mat Morgan. Bud's only hope was that, striking off to the south of Mat's cabin, and well away, he might intercept the outlaw on his way thither.

For that emergency his mind was braced. He had drawn the picture of Lucky Bill with such certainty that he knew the man as well as if he had known him for years. In the first place he was big. In the second place, his straw-colored hair was probably long enough to sweep his shoulders. His nose was "aquiline," which, according to the priest, meant crooked, like the beak of an eagle. In other words, it must be identical with the red, hooked nose of old Smithson, the blacksmith.

140

Gun Gentlemen

He had blue eyes, probably close together on either side of that cruel nose. Square jaws—no doubt an angle of unfleshed bone. His face was lean—therefore long, sunken-in cheeks and with Indian-high cheek bones. His mouth was not mentioned, but to fit in with the rest of that face it must be wide, thin-lipped. Such, then, was the goal of Bud's endeavors.

It would be false to say that Bud was not afraid; he was very much afraid. He recalled that the redoubtable sheriff himself had said that a man hunt was never over until someone was pumped full of lead. But Bud had limitless hopes. Such a big man would be an easy target, and he, Bud, would be equally small. That difference in size, he felt, ought to restore the balance in a great measure.

Having crossed the first range of hills and dipped into a broad valley beyond, Bud found a familiar little creek and stopped beside it to eat. It was well on into the afternoon, and he had not eaten since the daybreak breakfast. But he needed no elaborate meal. A piece of three-day-old bread, munched hastily, and a swallow of water was plenty of nourishment for Bud. There was something delightfully solemn in this first meal that he ate while on the trail of a man. In spite of himself he could not help lingering over the bread a little longer. The thrill of the thing was salt and meat to him.

And while he lingered there he heard the hooves of a horse scattering the stones on the far side of the hill to his left. Instantly he whisked onto the back of Pinto and sat in readiness, with his right hand on the butt of the heavy revolver. Then, over the crest of the hill, came a big cowpuncher who had just taken off his hat and was wiping his forehead with a handkerchief, so that the sun flashed and burned on a head of golden hair.

It was a pleasant thing to see, that and the big shoulders of the man, and the red bandanna fluttering at his throat. Also, Bud followed with a practiced eye of appreciation as the other's horse broke into a sharp trot downhill, weaving among the boulders, and the stranger swayed to the changing gaits with the easiest grace in the world. All in all, he was a very complete cavalier, and in the eyes of Bud he left little to be desired.

He saw the boy almost at once, but without checking the pace of his mount, he swung over to the left and came toward Bud. His horse halted close by.

"Where away, stranger?" asked the newcomer.

Bud completed a closer inspection of the horseman before he answered; he had a maxim from Sheriff Nevil that a wise man never hurries an answer. And although he had never seen a more prepossessing face or straighter pair of eyes than those of this man, he decided to hold himself well in reserve. And that was a maxim of his own.

"Oh," he said carelessly, "I'm going over yonder."

And he made a waving gesture which included a quarter of the points on the compass.

"I'm going about the same direction," said the stranger. "Shall we kill a bit of time together?"

It seemed to Bud that he should exhibit extra caution when he was on a man trail, but the good cheer of the other beat down the barriers.

"I dunno," he said slowly. "I don't mind if we do."

As the other started on, Bud ranged his horse beside him. Not exactly beside, either, but drawing a trifle toward the rear. Sheriff Nevil had told him that when in the slightest doubt about a stranger it was always well to keep one's horse a good neck to the rear. That made it possible to carry on a conversation without too much head turning, but it also gave one a strategic advantage of the most vital importance if trouble developed.

From this point to the rear he continued summing up the other. He noted the length of the arms, the capable hands, long-fingered and supple on the reins, and the cunning ease with which he kept the reins just taut enough to hold his horse in play. His big shoulders were carried well back, and there was a deep crease between the blades. The whole back of the man, indeed, bespoke the rippling muscles under his shirt.

A certain feeling of awe began to spread in Bud, although, as the sheriff often said, one could never judge a man until he'd been seen in action. It was the stranger who opened the conversation with a glance at Pinto.

"That hoss is pretty well set up," he said.

It was a most agreeable beginning to Bud, but he kept his pleasure out of his face.

"Oh, I dunno," he remarked nonchalantly. "I've seen a pile better."

In the meantime he examined the face of the other sharply, for the reply of the stranger hung a little at this retort from Bud. However, his face did not wrinkle in the faint beginnings of a smile—an expression which Bud had often seen in other men and which he detested above all things in the world. Instead, the big man looked him calmly and deeply in the eyes. So that it took Bud's breath a little, in fact.

"Maybe you have," he nodded. "I suppose I have, too. But I like them hind legs. Stifles angle out pretty well, and they's a nice, clean, wide hock. Nice bone, my friend; nice bone in them legs!"

It was wine and honey to Bud; another thing to soften his heart. This man did not call him "kid," and did not "jolly" him in that disgusting and light manner. Neither did he ask after his age, or whose boy he was, nor tell him that he was a bright-looking shaver. The absence of all these things meant more than silver-tongued oratory. To be referred to as "my friend" by that man's voice struck a chord in Bud that quivered for some moments.

"As a matter of fact," he admitted, "Pinto ain't so bad. Some that don't know him figure he's got a bad temper. What would you say?"

"I dunno," said the big man frankly. "I don't never set up to judge a man the minute I set eyes on him; or a hoss by the way he walks and throws his head. I won't say what I think his temper is, because I don't know."

It brought a smile of pleasure to Bud. In his knowledge of grown men, they were ashamed to admit ignorance or indecision on any subject whatsoever— particularly to one who happened to be a shade younger than themselves. Involuntarily he allowed Pinto to swing in closer to the stranger and to come up abreast of the other's horse.

"What I think," he confided earnestly, "is that when he was broke somebody slid a bur under the saddle. That's what's made him bad when he hears leather on his back."

"A skunk that would trick a hoss!" growled the big man.

Bud answered his look with one of equally friendly fierceness; another bond had fallen upon them.

"Some day," he said darkly, "I'll get the gent that done it!"

Then he glanced up quickly, for fear he might be

thought to have boasted. But there was no shadow on the other's face—such a shadow as falls when a man is keeping back a thought and a judgment. His eyes remained crystal clear.

They went on again for some time in silence, and Bud began to hunt desperately for a topic of conversation. For he did not know when their ways might part, and he felt that there were a thousand things which he would gladly hear about the inside of this man's mind.

Just to hear him talk was a pleasure. For his voice was both deep and gentle. Finally the other hitched his belt, and a topic occurred to Bud. He used it, for it was the best that he could think of.

"Don't that bother you none?" he asked. "Wearing your gun so far down on your hip? I should think maybe you'd want to have it in a saddle holster."

"Mostly gents do," agreed the other, "but I'm sort of partial to having this old gat in the same old place. I got it fastened to my leg so's it don't joggle up and down none to speak of, and it's always where I need it. Right under my hand."

"Well," admitted the boy, "that ain't a bad idea. I do the same. See?"

It was a motion he had practiced for hours, and one sweep of his hand up under his vest brought out the revolver. The other started a bit at the sight of it and looked quizzically at Bud. However, his expression was instantly controlled.

"I'll tell a man that's an old make—but, how d'you manage to get it out so dead easy from under that vest?"

"I'll tell you, it's just practice. Besides, this vest is so loose they's lots of room under it. It really ain't so hard as it looks. And—I didn't pull that gun to show off, stranger!''

There was something of an appeal in his voice, and the big man warmed to it instantly.

"Show off? Of course not. But it was a slick play. As I was saying, that's an old make.''

"This gun?'' said Bud carelessly, though he was now talking of the matter which lay nearest to his heart. "Yes, this old gun was made in '75.''

"You don't say!''

"Yep. I sure *do* say. Tell you how I know. You know when Custer died?''

"Not exactly. Why?''

"Nothing, except that it was in '76.''

"And what's that got to do with the gun. Mind saying?''

"Nothing much, except that this was one of the guns that Custer wore that day.''

"The hell you say! One of Custer's guns? Are you sure of that, friend?''

"Tolerable sure. My dad's brother was there that day.''

Chapter Fifteen

Judgment

It had all slipped out so easily—before he was aware, really. And the secrets which he had guarded from every one in the world were now in the possession of this stranger of a half hour's acquaintance!

He looked at the big man almost in fear, as one would look at a wizard who had looked into one's mind. Sheriff Nevil many a time had quizzed him about that gun, but he had kept back. For the weapon was sacred ground. He owned two things in the world. One was Pinto, which he had taken with his own hands. The other was the gun, which had come to him from his father, which he had oiled and tended and practiced with, whose touch he knew.

Yet the glance he cast at the stranger reassured him. The man was, indeed, different from other men.

147

"Mind if I look at it?" asked the big man.

"Sure, I don't," said Bud, and extended the gun. "But," he added, "I'd sort of rather you didn't handle it."

"Why—of course not if you say so."

"It's like this," said Bud hastily, and he flushed. "Not that I mind you taking hold of it, but I got a sort of superstition—I don't allow no man to take my gun from me while I can hang onto it."

"Between you and me, partner, that's a tolerable good idea."

"Besides," went on Bud, "just jogging along like this on hossback you couldn't hardly have a good look at a gun. And this one don't hang the same as most. It's got more weight in the barrel, you see? So they's some thinks it's top-heavy. But it ain't. Not a bit. You just got to know it, that's all."

He looked wistfully at the big man while he said this. Once he had voiced his philosophy of guns to the sheriff and had been received with laughter. But the new comrade—he who had just called him "partner"—was by no means amused. He nodded gravely.

"That's one of the truest words I ever heard a man say."

Bud turned the phrase in his mind with quiet delight—"a man!"

"Because," went on the other, "guns is like men. One man's friends ain't another man's friends. Every gent has his own likes and his own dislikes. You get used to the touch of a gun, and the way it hugs your hand, and that gun is the gun you want."

"It sure is," agreed Bud.

"I used to have an old gat that always carried low

Gun Gentlemen

and to the left—old secondhand gun—but I got to know its ways and make allowances. I carried that gun till it plumb wore out. That's a fact!''

"I believe it.''

"How about Custer's gun? Does it shoot straight?''

That question implied that every word Bud had spoken was believed. He felt a sort of choking gratitude to this free-hearted stranger.

"Sure it shoots straight,'' he answered. And out of the fullness of his heart he added: "Just gimme a mark.''

He regretted that speech an instant later, for he felt that men among men would not idly shoot at targets along the trail. But the big man did not smile or sneer.

"That black rock,'' he said, "with the red spot in the middle of it. That's a natural-made target.''

Instantly Bud's hand rose; the heavy gun exploded, and a white spot appeared on the rock. He held his breath, waiting with glistening eyes for a comment. For it was a good shot and a quick shot, and it was worthy of praise.

But this was what he heard: "No fault of the gun, I guess. You don't mind my suggesting something, eh?''

"Not a bit,'' said Bud faintly.

"You got a high right that time instead of hitting the center because you pulled with your trigger finger instead of squeezing with your whole hand.''

It was easy enough to talk!

"Maybe you'll show me what you mean?'' asked Bud a little sullenly.

"Sure. I'll try to,'' replied the other. And though they had passed the black rock by some yards, making a nasty angle for a shot at the face, he turned in the saddle toward it, and with a free, easy sweep of his hand brought

149

a .45 Colt out cocked and ready to fire. He held it loosely in the palm of his hand.

"Get my idea? You pull with your forefinger. My hunch is to squeeze with the whole hand like this. You close up on the butt and the trigger at the same time, and they ain't such a chance to throw the muzzle of the gun. Also, it always gives you a better grip and keeps your gun more in line if you miss the first time and have to shoot again. You see!"

He seemed to be looking more from the gun to Bud than from the gun to the target, but when the weapon exploded the red spot in the center of the face of the rock disappeared. An exclamation of wonder and delight rose to the lips of Bud, but he swallowed the words.

Instead, he looked the other in the eye, and said: "Say, I figure you could teach me a lot about shooting!"

The big man had already put up his weapon; there was no glint of triumph or amusement in his eye as he answered: "Not so much, either. You got a good fast eye and a steady hand. Them's the main things."

What a man among men he was! No wonder he had not praised that first shot; and what a triumph it would be, on some distant day when he, Bud, had mastered by assiduous practice that art of squeezing the gun, to hear the big man say: "Well, partner, you sure have improved."

The forward prospect made Bud tingle. And here would be a man to face the desperado, Lucky Bill! Then a sudden thought came to the boy. He pointed suddenly at his companion.

"Stranger, I know why you're here!"

He was rather surprised to see the other start; he had not thought that there were many things in this world that could make the big fellow's nerves jump.

"You know why I'm here? Well, out with it!"

Yes, there was a difference in his voice, too—a little ring of metal in it.

"You're here because of Lucky Bill!"

Again the start; Bud found the eyes of the other were squinting at him as though the big man wished to get inside his brain and read a secret there.

"What of it?"

"Oh, nothing."

"I suppose you're out here scouting for Lucky Bill yourself?" inquired the big man. At least, there was no contempt in his voice.

"Maybe I am," nodded Bud.

The other looked down at the ground, frowning; he seemed closed in solemn thought, and thought which was not altogether pleasant in nature.

"Well," he said slowly at length, "I'll say that I'm as much interested in Lucky as you are."

Bud chuckled. "I knew I'd guessed it! Well, I sure bet on you if you ever meet up with Lucky. But I hope I get the first crack at him."

"Never can tell."

"But I've got an idea that you'll get the five thousand."

"Five thousand?" cried the other, straightening, and with a surprise which seemed tinged with pain.

"Why, didn't you know? I guess you only heard that they was an offer of two thousand from the state. But besides that Mr. Aiken has put up three thousand more. Five thousand bucks—it ain't to be picked up every day. Price of fifty pretty fair sort of hosses, eh?"

The big man shuddered, and then he laughed in a

manner that sobered Bud oddly.

"The price of fifty hosses!" he said. "Who'd think that one man could be worth that much? Five thousand dollars dead or alive for Lucky Bill." He lowered his voice and added: "Well, this was coming to Lucky. He's killed more than one man.

"Well, he's a bad one, right enough. Yep, he's a murdering sort of a snake, I guess."

The big man stirred in his saddle—or perhaps it was merely the appearance of a twinge of pain.

"Do they say that about him?" he asked slowly. "A regular murderer?"

"Yep—a regular man-killer."

"Yet," said the other to Bud, "they's some say that Lucky Bill never took no advantage of any man he ever fought with. They's some say that he's always fought fair and square."

Bud scratched his head, but he found an answer not far from the surface.

"I leave it to you," he said. "Suppose I know I'm a lot faster on the draw and a lot straighter shooting with a gun than another gent, and I step up and insult him and make him go for his gat. I even let him make the first move, and then I get out my own gun and kill him easy before he's had a chance to pull his trigger. Ain't that murdering a man almost the same as shooting him when he don't have no gun in his holster at all?"

The big man moistened colorless lips. His voice had become husky.

"Every man that takes a chance with another gent's gun is taking a chance of dying quick," he said.

"Aw," chuckled Bud, "you're just saying that for the sake of talking me down. You know way down in your heart that I'm right, and that Lucky Bill is a murderer."

There was a pause.

"I wonder," said the big man so softly that it was hardly more than a whisper.

"Besides," said the boy, "you might talk away everything else he's done, but you couldn't talk away the killing of Harry Landrie. He done that with his hands. He beat Landrie to death, and he must of known what he was doing. Nope, that was plain murder.'

He was started to hear the unusual and mirthless laughter of the other again. It chilled his blood to hear it.

"Is they anything funny?" he asked uncertainly.

"Well," said the big man, "that was the last thing I ever thought would be held up against Lucky Bill. Why, I always thought Landrie was a sort of a crooked fighter and a damned snake!"

"You and me think the same thing," agreed the boy, "but when a gent is killed, murder is murder. Best man in the world and the worst—they ain't much difference in the way the laws looks at 'em. And what sort of a way would it be to live—having one gent favored over another? Ain't everybody got to have a chance?"

He found that the face of his companion was glistening with perspiration and his features were twisted up, as when one looks into a great distance.

"I put it up to you, partner, to see this another way."

Again that magic word, "partner." It warmed the blood of Bud.

"I'll tell you what," he said, "I'd *like* to see it your way if I could.'

"I think you would," said the other hurriedly, "and that makes it all the worse for Lucky Bill. Well, suppose you think about a gent that's chuck full of spirits and likes fun—and likes fighting more'n he does most other kinds of fun. And suppose he just naturally will fight with anything the other gent wants to fight with? Well, if he's in a place where they wear guns, ain't he apt to be fighting with guns? And if he fights with guns, ain't the fights apt to end up in killings or shot wounds? Is it his fault, then?''

''Seems like you're arguing pretty hard for this here Lucky Bill, you being one of them that's int'rested in him.''

''I'm interested in him as much as I am in any other man in the world.''

''You talk that way. I guess you're trying to make it seem right to hunt him down?''

''Maybe,'' muttered the big man.

''That's your way, all right,'' nodded the boy, and he smiled with a sudden openness of heart at his companion. ''You're a clean fighter and a straight shooter, all right. If I can't land him myself I hope you have the luck.''

''Thanks, and the same to you, friend.''

''Here's where I slope off in this direction. So long.''

''So long. Take care of yourself. And remember about squeezing the gun when you meet up with Lucky Bill.''

So they parted. And Bud didn't know that the big man, his new hero, was Lucky Bill himself.

Chapter Sixteen

The Trap

The boy darted off at a hard gallop, shifting his weight a little forward on his riding pad to ease the weight on Pinto. His loose-brimmed hat flared up in front, and his great vest flapped behind him; and Lucky Bill stared after him with a gloomy half smile. He was seeing himself in a far different light from that in which he had viewed his life and his past actions before he met the boy.

"Darn the kid," snarled Lucky sullenly.

But he added, as he turned his horse toward the trail that lay before them to Mat's shack: "I'm going to change. I'm going to cut it out."

Thoughtfully he pushed on across the hills until he struck out on the road west of Wheeler. And now, in a few minutes, he was within sight of the shack. A gloomy little house in a gloomy setting, and the sad light of the early evening was thickening over it. Here the creek which was dignified with the name of Sam's River, tumbled over a cliff to the northwest and spread out into a marshy flat.

To the southeast it picked up its strangled currents and drained out of the marsh again in a feeble, yellow stream. The marsh itself was hemmed in, upon three sides, by the ragged outlines of the cliffs—sometimes utterly inaccessible—sometimes stepping back in such a manner that it was barely possible for a man or even a horse to climb them. By this time, however, the evening was so dull that the cliffs looked to Lucky Bill like hills rather than flat-faced precipices.

Between the stretching arms of the cliffs in their sketchy semicircle rolled the willows of the marsh. Their yellow green was overtangled now by mists of delicate haze and a taint of blue as the night came early on the lowland. And half sheltered by the first range of shrubs and stubby willows was Mat Morgan's shack.

The road to Wheeler—or rather the dim, broad trail which went by the name of a road—dipped out of its straight course and folded in toward the shack, coming within a hundred yards of the building, and then straightened away west and east. Lucky Bill turned off the road and made for the hut.

As he did so there was an invisible stir behind the trees, and behind several little hummocks where the sheriff and his men were concealed. They had been waiting long and dreary hours for the coming of the fugitive. Many a time they had cursed him and their luck as they lay under the glaring sunlight, turning from side to side, or sprawling on their stomachs. But no matter how they rearranged their positions, the heat sifted through their clothes and began to burn the skin

Then came evening and coolness. But also there came with the shadows a certain conviction that the outlaw would never keep his appointment at Mat Morgan's place. Yet here he came, plainly visible. Every hand tightened around the balance of each rifle, and every eye squinted over the sights.

Any one of nine fingers might have beckoned ever so slightly and called forth the soul of Lucky; but the orders of the sheriff were definite—Lucky was not to be harmed until Mat had had a chance to draw from him information regarding the whereabouts of the girl. Otherwise who could tell where she was left, how guarded, how detained?

They saw the outlaw ride to the front of the hut, saw him dismount, and at the same time, as though a signal or a welcome to him, the hut bulged with light. A faint glow outlined the window; the door became a rectangle of yellow in which Lucky was outlined with murderous clearness for a second as he stepped into the house. Then the door closed, and there was only a pencil stroke of light at its top.

It consisted of one room for all purposes; there was the door and the one window—the window being more or less of a luxury. A new stove stood in one corner, a bunk was nailed to the opposite wall. There was a box and a chair. Otherwise the furnishings were negligible. Mat Morgan rose from the chair to welcome his visitor.

His face was quite colorless, perhaps from the loss of blood or from the passing of fever; and this pallor made his eyes seem larger and darker. But no doubt excitement accounted for part of this. He slipped between

Lucky and the door and closed it; instantly his one sound hand was clutched in the shoulder of the larger man.

"And Molly?" he whispered. "Molly?"

"What's the matter? Why the whisper, Mat? Anybody near enough to hear?"

That random shot told more than he could guess, but he attributed the sudden pinching up of Mat's face to a twinge of pain from his hurt shoulder.

"Sit down, Mat," he insisted. "Sit down and rest yourself. Don't be rollicking around with a bum arm."

"My arm ain't so bad," said Mat darkly. "And one arm is still good."

There was no particular point in this assertion. Fearing that his pride had made him too defiant, he swung back to the topic of the girl.

"But where's Molly? Didn't you bring her, Lucky?"

The other drew the box between his legs and sat down, tilting his shoulders against the wall. He pushed up the brim of his hat, and the light from the lamp glinted on the bronze of his cheeks and the white of his forehead. He was watching Mat Morgan with an intent thoughtfulness.

"I guess it's been pretty hard on you waiting here all this time, Mat?"

"I thought you'd be along this morning at the latest. Sure it's been hard waiting. Worse'n waiting for a train. But you didn't get her, Lucky?"

The latter smiled. "You're pretty much on edge. Ain't hard to see you're pretty fond of her, partner."

"Damn it, yes, of course I'm fond of her—crazy about her. But where is she?"

Lucky had developed a maddening way of dodging these direct questions.

"I got her well enough," he said. "Not such an easy time, either."

"But you have her. That's the main thing. Thank goodness for that, Lucky. Is she outside?"

"Sit down. Don't rush. I got her, but it was some fight. She didn't trust what I said about coming from you. Had to make her come by force. Then Landrie bumped into us on the trail. The skunk wouldn't work with a gun. We had to fight with fists. Well, in the end he took a fall and hit his head on a rock and passed out."

"You mean," said Mat Morgan with a sinister grin, "you slammed him on the head with a rock and he passed out. Go on, Lucky."

"I mean what I say," asserted the other firmly, "and nothing else. I fought him fair and square with my fists. If I'd wanted to kill the hound wouldn't I of used my gun?"

"Sure you would," nodded Mat with an unbelieving smile. "Go on."

"I got the girl away; she come willingly enough after that."

"Scared of you, maybe? Scared maybe you'd be using your fists on her the next thing?"

Lucky winced.

"Maybe it was that. I don't think that was the only thing, though. She seemed kind of reasonable. Didn't mind me talking to her. You know she'd always hated Landrie?"

"Yep. But where did you cache her away? And how've you made sure that she'll stay where you put her?"

"Because I promised her that if she ran away I'd fol-

159

low her to the end of the world and bring her back to you again.''

Mat Morgan was moved. He had trapped Lucky Bill in his own house; and for the very reason that he had wronged the man shamefully and without cause, he hated Lucky from the bottom of his heart. In spite of that hatred he was stirred now.

''You're the kind of a gent to have for a partner, Lucky. It was sure a lot to do for a gent you'd never known much about.''

''I guess you're worth it all,'' said Lucky. ''I guess you are.''

His voice implied that he might have some small doubts on this subject, and that he was now reassuring himself.

''Seeing,'' he added, ''that it all hangs on how much you care for her.''

''I'm crazy enough about her,'' admitted Mat Morgan, ''if that's what bothers you. But you couldn't bring her on to see me here? Was she too tired?''

''Yes,'' said the outlaw gently. ''Kind of tired out.'' He searched for a way to communicate his painful tidings to the lover. ''Queer how women are, Mat. They're ready to start pretty near anything, and they go out with a jump and a run. Inside of a mile they're tired out and hate the thing they started after—or they say that they do. Same way with their minds. They start to like a thing and then they break off and hate it the next minute. They ain't nothing constant about 'em.''

At this Mat Morgan looked closely at his companion.

''Have you got any special meaning behind that, Lucky?''

The big man looked sadly at him.

"I been trying to break it to you easy, Mat, but I guess I'm a bum diplomat."

Mat Morgan rose.

"Spit it out."

"Mat, she ain't meant for you; she's changed her mind."

There was a swift and fierce struggle in the face of Mat Morgan; then he controlled himself.

"Go on. Tell it all out."

"She started out thinking she was pretty fond of you. But chiefly she hated Landrie and wanted to get away from him. It was you rather than him. But now that he's out of the way, she finds that she don't fancy you quite so much, Mat, old man."

Mat Morgan came a slow step toward Lucky, looking intently at him. He paused, and oddly enough his sound left hand settled around the lamp and the fingers gripped it hard. It was very much as though he trembled on the verge of hurling the lamp at the head of Lucky. So vivid was the illusion that Lucky teetered forward on his box and gathered his feet beneath him, alert.

"Maybe," said Mat softly, "she favors somebody else more?"

"Maybe she does. They ain't no telling what goes on inside her head."

"And maybe that somebody is you?"

"Me? What put that fool idea in your head, Mat?"

"Talk straight, Lucky. Here I am with a bum right arm. You ain't afraid to tell the truth to me now, I guess? Here I am alone and helpless, Lucky."

He sneered as he spoke, and Lucky answered with a frown: "I'd talk straight to you if you had ten arms, son. What is it?"

"You've gotten pretty much interested in the girl, eh?"

"I love the ground she walks on."

The directness of that answer staggered the other.

"You took your time, Lucky. You picked your chance when I was down and out to talk sweet to her and win her over. You're pretty fast with your hand, Lucky, and I guess you're still faster with your tongue, eh?"

In his turn Lucky rose. He seemed very big, and behind him his shadow leaped up and dwindled as the flame rose and fell in the throat of the chimney.

"You get this straight, Mat. I give you my word that I'd get that girl for you, and I've got her. You think I've been talking soft to her? I tell you straight, I ain't whispered one wrong thing. I'd rather cut out my tongue first. I ain't run you down, and I ain't run myself up. I been working for you, and I'm still going to work for you, no matter what you are."

It shook Mat Morgan.

"Are you meaning that?" he asked.

"I ain't one that plays tricks with words," declared Lucky scornfully. "I don't have to," he added with pride. "But here's my point: Molly Aiken don't love you no more. D'you insist on having her in spite of that?"

"What difference does it make what she thinks today so long as she thought another way yesterday? Ain't you said yourself that they's always changing? Tomorrow she'll be head over heels in love with me, Lucky. Anyway, I'll take a chance on it!"

He ground his teeth in anger.

"Take your time, Mat," said the other. "I ain't persuading you. But don't do nothing rash where they's a woman mixed up in it. Them kind of things ain't never properly undone once they're done.''

"My mind is set like a rock."

He watched Lucky passing through a silent struggle.

"She's been bought and paid for," said Lucky grimly, more to himself than to his companion. "They's been one man killed already, and the chances is they'll be more trouble. She belongs to Mat."

"And what are you going to do about it?"

"I'm going to take you where I left her."

"Bring her to me, partner." Mat had lowered his voice to persuasiveness. "Lucky, I been saying some hard things, but that's because it ain't hard for me to get suspicious when Molly is in the talk. But bring her here. You see I ain't in any fit shape to go a-courting her."

"I'd do what you say," answered Lucky, "but I want you to let me off. I'll tell you why, Mat. I couldn't hardly trust myself if I was to see her again. I've had a thousand funny kind of things on the tip of my tongue to say to her. If I was to see her again I got an idea that all them things would come tumbling out and I'd make a fool of myself."

"Or out of me," suggested Mat coldly.

Lucky was perfectly frank. "Maybe," he admitted. "You never know which way a girl is going to jump. She's like a two-year-old being rid for the first time."

"Tell me where she is," said Mat Morgan, making up his mind, "and I'll go fetch her."

"I'll take you there. Get your things on, partner, and we'll start."

"I got an idea I'll wait till the morning. Just tell me where to find her, Lucky, and I'll do the rest."

"I thought you was plumb on edge to see her," said

the big man quizzically, "and here you are putting it off."

A womanish temper had been rising in the other during all the interview, and now it burst out unreasonably: "Are you going to tell me where she is, or ain't you?"

"I dunno," growled Lucky. "I don't exactly like that line of talk, partner, and now I come to think about it, I got my doubts about telling you where she is—under compulsion. You come with me to find her, and you come right now. If you don't care that much about her—why, be damned to you!"

The lips of Mat Morgan twitched. Once more his left hand settled around the lamp, but changing his mind, so it seemed, he merely turned and placed the lamp on the box, so that it shone through the exact center of the window.

Chapter Seventeen

Riding Through

When he turned again his face was composed. It was better, after all, that Lucky Bill should reach the end of his course at once, he had decided. For with a touch of premonition he began to feel that Lucky himself was the reason for the girl's change of mind.

Not only because of his own hatred of the man, but because of the girl, it was time for Lucky Bill to die. Besides, if he lived ever so little longer, was it not possible that he would be able to explain away the death of Harry Landrie?

"They ain't any use of talking longer," he said to Lucky. "We're just getting heated up with words. So long, partner. Thanks for what you've done for me; but I'll try to get along without you from now on. For the last time, will you tell me where the girl is?"

He fixed his eyes upon the outlaw; but with all his mind he was listening for some sound from outside the house. The sheriff must have seen the signal of the light in the window by this time, and he would be approaching with his men. There was not a sound to be heard. Nevil and his party must be stalking like Indians. A consuming anxiety seized upon Mat Morgan to get Lucky out of the room, for if the fight occurred here there was no question that Lucky's first bullet would be for the man who had betrayed him.

"For the last time," said Lucky, "I won't tell you where she is. Come on with me, or give her up. You understand? If you drop this now, if you stay here, I consider I got a free hand."

He was on fire with excitement as he spoke.

"Do what you please," said Mat coldly. "Good night."

Lucky nodded, settled his hat over his eyes, and without a word strode to the door. There he whirled and found Mat looking out the window.

"Mat!"

"Well? Still here?"

"Seems like you're tolerably interested in that window."

"You ain't talking sense, Lucky."

The big man walked straight up to him.

"You smile too much, Mat. I don't trust no man that smiles too much. What's behind your smile?"

"Are you trying to pick a fight? D'you want to get me out of your way—is that it?"

"It's something about the way you looked after you moved the lamp. I dunno what, but—Mat, for your sake I've got a price on my head, and I'm meat for any man's gun. Maybe you'd like to have part of five thousand dollars for yourself.''

"I don't foller you."

"You don't know they's a price on me?"

"Never heard a word about it."

"When did you leave Wheeler?"

"Last night, of course."

"Have you had anything to eat today?"

"What d'you mean, Lucky?"

"Talk sharp!"

"Sure. I had something this afternoon."

"Coffee?"

"Sure."

"Mat, you lie like a snake. They's dust all over the top of that stove. It ain't been used today! You lie. You're full of lies. Now, what's it all mean? And that lamp—''

Mat Morgan had retreated little by little during this last speech, followed not by the body of Lucky Bill, but by the hardening and lowering of his voice. Now his shoulders struck the wall, and as though that contact unnerved him with surprise, showing that it was impossible for him to retreat farther, the last vestige of color was suddenly swept from his face. To keep his lip from trembling he held it firm with his teeth. He was a picture of terror. And Lucky Bill watched him half in bitter scorn and half in hatred.

"What a skunk you are, Mat!" he said savagely, "I'd ought to drill you clean, but I can't do it! You've trapped me, eh? Well—I'll take my chance. But when you got two arms, and when you're around sound and safe again, watch for me, Mat, because as sure as my name's Bill, I'm coming back to get you!''

He sprang to the window, caught up the lamp, and dashed it to pieces on the floor at Mat's feet.

In place of the steady glow of the lamp there was a blur of darkness, then a wild and flickering light as the burning oil swept across the floor. In that first breath of darkness Lucky slipped through the window with the terrified yell of Mat Morgan ringing after him.

He landed on the sandy ground outside, crouched and ran for his horse. And at the same time he saw figures rise out of the night, looking vaster than ordinary men. There were half a dozen flashes and reports, and bullets hummed behind him and ate into the wood of the cabin.

They had fired at the window which a moment before had been illumined, and then had been so surprisingly blanketed with darkness through which Lucky had jumped. So certain had seemed their surprise that the sudden change caught them off balance—as if a prize fighter, set far back to drive home the finishing punch at a staggering opponent, should be hit unexpectedly in the face.

Again the darkness of the hut was now replaced by a wild and flickering light which was worse than none at all, so far as shooting was concerned. One moment light was flung in their faces and upon the fugitive. The next a wave of darkness covered everything, as the oil in the room, during the first few seconds, sputtered, sent up a leaping flame, and then the dark, until the fire should get under way.

Starlight alone would have been enough for any one of them to riddle Lucky by, but they had not even starlight to help them. It was like having a lantern flashed in their eyes. They were blinded, made uncertain.

In the meantime Lucky had found the saddle with a

sprawling leap. Lights were winking before him as the
startled posse worked their repeaters. A loose semicircle
of shooting men. One glance told him the lay of the land.
There was no escape by way of the road and the open
country beyond, and he swerved his horse and sent it
crashing into the willows.

Behind him a confused yelling of oaths—and a rapid
fire of well-directed shots. But though the bullets
combed the trees around him, his proverbial good fortune stood him in stead. He was not touched, and his
horse went scatheless.

Then, as he spurred the horse forward, they struck the
soft marshland and the animal floundered heavily. Lucky
drew rein and spurred the mustang back onto firm
ground. Then he set about taking more accurate stock of
his surroundings.

Out beyond the trees a loud voice which he recognized as the voice of Mat Morgan was shouting: "You
got him, boys. He can't get up the bluffs. I know. Scatter
out. Settle down. He's got to come out on this side."

Lucky looked back through a break in the willows at
the semicircle of the cliffs. It was not light enough for
him to see them in detail, of course, but he took Mat
Morgan's word for their steepness. It was a neat trap,
and a tighter one than he had ever been in his life.

The flames from the burning shack were rising higher
now, and long shafts of quivering light were thrust
through the willows, withdrawn, and sent lunging far
into the darkness again. Obviously they would not follow him into the forest by night, and with the thought a
rash plan came to the fugitive.

No doubt they pictured him plunging deeper and
deeper into the marshland, making for the cliffs oppo-

site. What if he should turn and attempt to take the guards by surprise and run the gauntlet?

Once before he had slipped through their fingers, and the gambling fever which makes a man bet again, high, on the cards with which he has bluffed and won before, took hold on Lucky. At any rate, he could go back and survey the chances.

He pushed his horse cautiously to the verge of the willows and peered out.

The shack was now a black shell of a house with the fire roaring up through the roof and eating holes in the sides. In a few more minutes it would collapse with a crash. It furnished, in the meantime, enough light for him to mark the forms of the men of the posse scattering out in a loose-flung line.

Instinctively they had taken it for granted that the outlaw would not attempt to immediately try that most dangerous line of escape, and above all they seemed to feel that he would not break out at the exact spot of the burning house where the light would make him a most tempting target, clearly defined. Accordingly, they had worked out down the outer line of the willows.

Another thing which he noted was that they were on foot. Later on they would doubtless send one of their number for the horses, and he would distribute them again; in the meantime the widely scattered units of the posse certainly lacked mobility of movement.

But to attempt to break out on the very verge of the burning house, where the light of the conflagration would plainly illumine him for well over a hundred yards of his flight! It took the breath of even Lucky Bill. Yet he worked his horse along behind the screening trees until he was exactly opposite the house, and choosing a moment when the nearest of the guards had turned his back to move farther off, he sent the mustang into a trot.

A gallop was the natural choice. A gallop was the thing for which every nerve in his body was tingling; but Lucky knew that a swift-moving object will attract the eye ten times more quickly than one which travels slowly. Besides, each one of those guards must be set in expectation of a man plunging out of the willows at the top speed of his horse.

So Lucky Bill moved the mustang forward with tightened reins.

The fire served him in at least one way—the spread of flames and smoke shut him off from the view of the entire left wing of the posse, and the nearest man on the right was walking in the opposite direction. He was opposite the flames now, then out on the farther side he heard a yell taken up and repeated down the line. They had seen him!

His spurs went home with the first quaver of that cry; with the first jump of the horse the rifles began to crackle with hysterical speed, but Lucky was flattened along the back of his mount, gaining speed with every jump. The bullets sang close, but the kindly dimness began to gather around him.

It was over like the blinding rush of a wind; the yells and the shooting fell away as though he had turned a corner. Looking back, Lucky saw them rushing for their horses, and he laughed to himself, for he knew his mount.

Chapter Eighteen

The Discovery

Some brushwood, half dead and dry, but green enough to burn with a disgusting amount of smoke, was the fire for Bud that night. Not that he had any need of fire to cook with, for his food was of the nature which needs no preparation. But he felt that the trail would not be the trail if he did not conform to the proprieties, at least so far as to build his fire at night. So he sat over it until the smoke had choked him, filled his nostrils with soot, and burned his eyebrows and stung his eyes until the tears ran down his cheeks.

He pretended to himself that he enjoyed all this. He had often heard men describe the flicker of the campfire at night and how friendly the wavering of a flame may be to a lonely man. Conscientiously, therefore, he tended the fire. He looked out upon the hills and made himself feel that they were black and cold and friendly. As a matter of fact, he felt that he knew them as well as he knew the face of any man. He had a glance for the stars also. In fact, he felt that he was comporting himself in all respects as a man on the death trail should act.

Pinto, however, worried him greatly, for the mustang insisted on lying down behind him like a dog, and certainly this was no addition to the dignity of either horse or master. Yet it was very comforting to see that familiar head and the bright, round eyes, so intelligent, so knowing of the master. He could not help patting the shining neck, and yet he despised himself for it.

On the trail one's horse should be simply a machine—so many pounds of useful muscle to be thrown away in a cruel and prolonged burst of running, if necessary.

He sat back a little, coughing, and tried to rally his thoughts to the problem which was before him. He was desperately tired and sleepy, but he knew that every man on the trail rallies himself and, before he sleeps, makes his plans for the coming day. In his mind there was unrolled a clear picture of the whole district, and every house was spotted in his memory. Over that mental map he pored and studied. Somewhere Lucky Bill was hidden, and in that place was a treasure of five thousand dollars.

It seemed less easy now to meet the outlaw hand to hand. The big man of the trail from whom he had separated that afternoon had filled him with respect for fighting men; at the most he only hoped now to be able to locate the hunted man and lead the men of the law to him. In that case they might give him a large percentage of the spoils. At the least, it would give him reputation.

Bud coughed again and changed to a third position.

Somewhere in that district was Lucky Bill. Where? After all, there were only so many definite possibilities. The sheriff was sure he would find Lucky at Mat Morgan's house; the big man was equally sure to hunt in a different place. Both of them were confident, and both might be wrong. He, Bud, had an equal chance of discovering the truth. A cloud of smoke rolled out, climbed up his bare shanks, rolled into his face, and set him sneezing. He struck into it with his open hand furiously. And then he stood up.

"Smoke always comes where you ain't expecting it," growled Bud, scowling at his fire.

This time he sat down farther off. The smoke was like Lucky Bill; it took people by surprise. And why? Instead of hunting for clues to Lucky Bill, why not look first in the place where it would seem least probable that he had found a shelter.

The idea was an inspiration. Bud became excited. Where in the district was the least likely shelter for Lucky Bill? Where was the least likely hiding place for any man?

In the plain, open country, perhaps? That was an idea over which he dwelt for some time. Suppose the hunted man had simply camped out in the hills, taking his chance on being found and on seeing his trailers before they saw him? Yet other people had done this and had been caught. The mind of Bud roamed over places where he himself would never have dreamed of going to hide, and finally his thought came, with a shudder, to the haunted house of old Taliaferro.

There, certainly, was the least likely place of all. He, Bud, would rather face the muzzles of ten guns than rap at the door of that house. But for that very reason a peculiar certainty grew up in him that this was the place where the outlaw had hidden. His mind worked, naturally enough, by the law of opposites; the more he grew cold at the thought of the haunted house, the more certain he was that Lucky had gone there.

He must abandon all thought of rest this night, he saw, and go to test the truth of his idea. It was a harsh trial for Bud. The mountains had become black and lonely and shapeless; his dying fire gave a wretched light and set the eyes of Pinto glimmering through the darkness. And then he thought of the stories of old Taliaferro which had come to him—the gaunt old man with the ready shotgun. And perhaps, so the story went, he was not really a man at all, but a malignant ghost who guarded some guilty secret in the haunted house.

Bud closed his eyes and groaned.

How comfortable and warm to be now in bed in Wheeler, in the attic over the haymow which was his house and home! And why not return? No one knew why he had set forth. No one would reproach him. No one could point the finger of shame at him.

"But," said Bud to himself, "the worst things that can happen to a gent is to know more bad things about himself than other folks know. It ain't what the others say; it's what a gent says to himself."

After a while he closed both hands hard. "I ain't afraid," declared Bud to the boundless night.

With his teeth set he started to get Pinto ready for another journey, and had to kick the mustang with his bare toes until they ached before the wise horse would get up. "That ain't a good sign," moaned Bud to himself. "Pinto don't want to go. Maybe he knows more'n I do."

But Pinto finally lurched to his feet with a disgusted grunt, and in another moment they were journeying across the plain and toward the southwestern hills. It was the swiftest trip that Bud ever made in his life. The miles seemed to fly away of their own volition. And he was carried with a grim speed straight to the environs of the haunted house. At a little distance he drew rein, swallowing, because his throat was dry, and twisting his hands together to restore the circulation of his cold blood.

The moon shone on the haunted house. It made the roof white and the sides jet-black. It showed the ancient outhouses tumbles of black and white. Every broken doorway, every empty window of those ruins, made to Bud a yawning mouth of danger. The ghoulish old man might be lurking in any one of them and watching the approaching victim with silent and fiendish laughter.

Of one thing Bud was perfectly sure: that if he had to face the old man he would be powerless to lift a hand or stir a foot. It was madness, therefore, to stay near the house, but one thing in Bud was almost greater than his terror, and that was his disgust with himself.

Briefly, he called up the stern faces of his heroes—Watkins, who had been captured by five Indians, had cut his bonds and killed them all with a single knife and escaped; Captain Preston, who disguised himself and was actually able to mingle with a party on the warpath as one of their number until he could destroy them. These faces came in the night and looked in upon the trembling soul of Bud. They could not despise him more than he despised himself.

Dismounting, he stole with great caution among the buildings. Every footstep must be watched, for the ground was littered with dead, rotted wood. And the turning of every corner must be accomplished with infinite, patient caution. So he came at length around the end of a crumbled barn and found the house in full view.

It seemed huger than any building he had ever seen at this close range. Its size made it more formidable. It seemed impossible that any flesh-and-blood creature should by preference live behind those black and eyelike windows. Only a ghost belonged in the dusty halls, and the vast, ruinous rooms.

Go nearer to that building? Bud would far rather have faced a leveled revolver; yet he must go on.

He was about to step forward when a very light and whispering sound came to him from one side, and turning, he saw, to his infinite horror, a slowly moving figure wrapped in perfect white—a filmy white, which showed in the moonshine like a mist.

Bud shrank, half sick with fear, into the steep and narrow shadow along the side of the barn. But the figure was coming straight toward him. He had been seen? No; the ghost paused, looked up, and seemed to regard the moon fixedly, and in so doing the white shawl which had covered its head rippled away to the shoulders.

Bud, to his infinite relief and amazement, found himself looking into the face of a pretty girl. She was amazingly and delightfully flesh and blood. From the luster of her eyes to her half smile, which seemed very sad to Bud, there was nothing about her that did not please him. He looked after her in a sort of happy trance, while she went to the house and disappeared through the back door.

Bud was on the verge of rising to follow her when the truth broke in on him. Miraculously he had been right. This was the shelter of Lucky, for yonder girl could be no other than Molly Aiken. The sheriff must know of it. He turned and scampered, his fear all gone, back to Pinto, and, mounting, he turned the head of the tough mustang toward the Wheeler trail.

Chapter Nineteen

Taliaferro Advises

When men are disappointed in one bright hope they do not readily turn to another; when Lucky Bill slipped through the line of the posse so unexpectedly they gave him up at once. There was a half-hearted pursuit, but by the time they had got their horses he was out of sight among the hills, and they never regained a glimpse of him in the night.

He rode at top speed for a short time, and then held back the mustang to a dogtrot. Instinctively he had taken the trail to the house of old Taliaferro. It was not that he saw clearly what he could do there, but he had a vague idea that he owed something to the girl. He had taken her there; perhaps it would be right for him to bring her back again to the house of her father.

At least he could offer his assistance, and if the girl,

as seemed probable, should refuse his offer with scorn, there would be no harm done. He tried to understand her and her sudden change of mind; and he found that it was actually pleasant to be confronted by a mystery.

Yet as he approached the old house, late that night, he experienced a sudden falling of the heart, a sense of guilt, as though what he had done made him susceptible to her reproaches.

His horse, as though he recognized his last place of rest, raised his head and neighed loudly. It sent a qualm through the outlaw, and he cut the sound short by reining in hard with a touch of the spurs that made the mustang leap forward. He put the animal up in the shed which it had occupied before, and came back to the house, as black and solemn of face as it had been on that first night when he stopped before it with Molly Aiken. A great time seemed to have elapsed since then—enough, at least, to separate him from the girl by a distance which he could not yet judge.

To his great astonishment, the door opened at his first uncertain tap, and he saw old George, lamp in hand, with his white curl glowing like a halo and the light wrinkling over his grin.

"Mas' Jeff'son is done expecting you, suh," said the negro.

"Expecting me?" growled Lucky, trying to peer past the smile and get at the meaning of it.

"This way, suh."

He followed to the sanctum of old Taliaferro, and found that worthy ensconced as usual between the wings of his big chair, with the red of a dying fire pleasantly staining his face, and the meager hands which were folded beneath his chin. He rose and bowed profoundly.

"We have been expecting you," he said. "Come in."

The friendly greeting completely unnerved the cowpuncher. He was prepared for locked doors and guns behind them, just as he had left the house, but now it was as if he had ridden away leaving smiles behind him. He took a chair and slipped slowly into it, never allowing his eye to diverge from the withered form of the master of the house.

"We?" he repeated. "Who's we?"

"Miss Aiken and I," replied Taliaferro. "She has been sitting here with me."

Again Lucky was stunned. "I'm glad," he said, "that there's no hard feelings."

"Hard feelings?" echoed his companion, waving such a thought into limitless oblivion. "Why should there be? We are rejoiced to welcome you back. But first—you are tired and hungry."

"Not a bit. I was a minute ago. Now I feel on the top of the world."

And he smiled frankly at his host. The latter regarded him benevolently.

"There is a certain openness," he moralized, "which I have always considered a high type of diplomacy."

This point passed over the head of Lucky, and the observant old man brought the conversation to a humbler level.

"And now the result of your mission?" he asked. "Can you tell me about that?"

"About Mat Morgan?" repeated Lucky uncomfortably. "Well, he won't give her up. I told him she'd changed her mind, but he won't give her up."

"You still intend to bring her to him?"

"No. They's been a pile of things happened; and the

181

chief thing that come out is that Mat's a skunk!''

"Ahh!" sighed Mr. Taliaferro.

"He laid a trap for me. Here was I trying to help him, and there was him getting ready to turn me over to the law."

"The law?"

"Partner," said Lucky, "I dunno what you know about all this."

"Nearly everything, I think."

"Then you know they got a price on my head? Five thousand?"

The other made no rejoinder, and Lucky, in his honesty, confessed the whole.

"Which means, Mr. Taliaferro, that you are liable to the law for giving me shelter. I dunno what they can do to you, but it'd probably be a pile."

Still the little old man made no reply, until at length he got out of his chair and formally proffered his hand to Lucky.

"From the first," he said, "I knew you were no common man; but I am rejoiced to have under my roof a man who is worth five thousand dollars—to the law!"

He resumed his seat while Lucky was still winking.

"In my family," he continued, "this distinction has been not infrequently conferred, and various members have been at random times pursued by anything from a troop of horses to a squadron of his majesty's ships. Therefore, make yourself entirely at home. We are no longer strangers, sir."

"If we ain't strangers," said the blunt Lucky, "maybe you'll tell me what happened that made you take down a gun for me this morning?"

"The simplest thing in the world. I would have done

no less to my own brother. The lady told me she no longer wished to accompany you on your journey to Mat Morgan. And I thank heaven that the Taliaferros have always been at the service of women and servants of their wishes.

"If you had broken down the door I humbly assure you that I would have driven two charges of buckshot into your body. I am glad to say that you did not break down the door. But to a man of your caliber it was obviously impossible that you should enter the room against the will of the lady."

At this the lower jaw of Lucky thrust out a little. And there was a glitter of anger in his eyes.

"Partner," he drawled, "you and me don't come out of the same time. The way you see it, what a woman wants is law. The way I see it, right is right, no matter what something in skirts says about it."

"A grave point of difference."

"The way I figure it now, since I can't take her on to Mat Morgan, I'm sure going to take her back to her father."

"She, perhaps, may have something to say on that subject."

"She'll most like say a whole pile. But what she'll do is the main thing; and what she'll do is to come along with me."

"A rather brutal attitude, my young friend."

"It's for her good You think I can leave her drifting around the country like this? No; back she's got to go."

He discovered that his warmth had not communicated itself to his host. The latter was even smiling benefi-cently upon him.

"If I were a gambling man, I'd bet you a round sum

on that," murmured Mr. Taliaferro. "Unless you are entirely blind."

"Blind? Now, what d'you mean by that?"

"Lucky Bill, why do you think that she refused to continue the journey to Mat Morgan?"

"I dunno. Just a whim. I can't explain why the sun comes up or the earth turns, for that matter."

"Do you know what she said when you rode away this morning?"

"Sure. 'Thank heaven he's gone.' She most like said that in girl talk."

"On the contrary, she said: 'He must be terribly angry. Do you think he is?' Does that tell you something, Lucky?"

"It tells me something I knew before. That girls is queer."

The old man burst into causeless laughter, irritating Lucky.

"During the day she often wondered if you would ever come back. And this evening she sat there in the same chair in which you are now sitting."

Lucky started.

"And when she heard a horse neigh a little while back, she jumped up with her face on fire. 'It's Lucky,' she said in such a voice that I can hear it tingle still in my ears."

"Was she as mad as that?" groaned Lucky.

"Mad? Well, sir, I don't know how the young men are raised in these degenerate times, but I did not think that she was exactly angry.

"Well, I said to her, 'Now you'll have a chance to tell him what you think.'

" 'I?' she cries at me, as though she were frightened.

Gun Gentlemen

'I wouldn't dream of facing him.'

"And off she goes, helter-skelter, to her room. And that's why she isn't here waiting for you."

"But what does it all mean if it don't show she's mad at me?" muttered Lucky.

The old man suddenly exploded.

"You infernal young idiot, it means that she's in love with you!"

"What!" gasped Lucky.

"Go to her tomorrow morning and take her in your arms."

"What!"

But Mr. Taliaferro seemed to have forgotten his guest. He was smiling into the past.

"In the old days," he said, "the youth of the nation were of a different cast."

Chapter Twenty

The Second Clue

Daybreak over Wheeler found the posse and the sheriff in a sound sleep. They had worked hard the day and the night before, and now they had earned a rest. Before the first light an active little figure in loose vast and ragged knee trousers had rushed to the door of the sheriff's house and attempted to enter, and had been flung bodily out by the negro at the door.

"But I got to see him," cried Bud. "It means—it means taking Lucky Bill!"

It was like talking to an ear of stone. The servant had received most definite orders and dared not admit any one until the sheriff had had his sleep out. And when Bud found that he could not have access to Nevil, he went back to Pinto in the shed, crawled into the hay-mow, bunched himself with his knees under his chin,

186

and with one last wriggle to fit himself into the sagging hay, he was instantly fast asleep.

Noon came burningly upon the village of Wheeler, and then the sheriff wakened. He ate breakfast with Mr. Aiken, both in a gloomy silence until the second cup of coffee.

"When we get him," exploded the rancher at length, "I want you to wink, sheriff. Because I intend to hang him to the highest tree within ten miles of Wheeler and let the buzzards have him."

"Here's the point," said the calm sheriff, "what do you most want: to get your girl back, or to hang Lucky Bill?"

"He's balked me twice," said the rancher, answering indirectly. "Twice I've had him in gun range, and twice he's gotten off scot-free! Confound the girl! Give her enough rope, and she'll run in a circle and come home again. But this desperado has to be done for, once for all. He's a public menace."

"He's a menace to me," admitted the sheriff. "He's put a hole in my reputation that you could drive a pair of horses through. But I'd rather that Mat had learned where the girl is."

"Is Morgan square?"

The sheriff smiled. In a way, it was reply enough.

"Least said, the better. What d'you aim to do now, Mr. Aiken?"

"Stay on this trail until I've got the hide of Lucky Bill. Sheriff, that fellow's skin is charmed! When he broke out from the trees, I got a dead bead on him as he shot his horse past the burning shack. I couldn't miss. I had the sight hugging him. And when I pulled on the trigger I wouldn't of traded his life for a sack of nuts.

But when I looked again he was still riding.''

"Firelight is tricky stuff to shoot by. Better luck next time.''

A silence fell between them, and they stirred the sugar into the black coffee.

"After all,'' muttered the sheriff at length, "the kid was right. Lucky came to Mat's place.''

"Who is the kid?''

"I dunno, exactly. He just sort of happened along. Well, they say his folks lived over to Bruno and they both died, and he didn't have nothing to claim him. He wandered along to Wheeler.''

"And the town sort of adopted him?''

"Adopt Bud?'' chuckled the sheriff. "They ain't enough men in Wheeler to adopt Bud, and they ain't no one man in the world big enough for the job. No, he's just hung around and done chores for his grub. He can swing a rope like a growed-up man. He's a nice hand with a rifle, and he'd be a fine one with a revolver if he had a bit more weight in his arm. Yep, he's a promisin' kid, is Bud, and he'll be a credit to Wheeler if he don't burn up the town with one of his tricks some day. Here's the sky pilot.''

By this irreverent expression he referred to the priest, as Father Connell came into the room.

"But what beats me,'' said the sheriff, after the new-comer had sat down, "is how you can be so blame cheerful!''

"Would you have expected me to rejoice?'' asked Father Connell. "If the man had been taken, and killed, would you have expected me to be happy?''

"A burr is a burr,'' said Aiken, "and I don't give a hang what becomes of it until it gets under my saddle blanket. Then I want to get rid of it, quick. Lucky Bill is the burr under my saddle now."

They were eating in the dining room of the Empire Hotel, and now the sheriff saw a familiar, tattered figure leaning in the door.

"Hallo! Bud!" he called. "Come in and have something with us."

Bud sauntered slowly across the room, took in the sheriff and his guests with a curt nod, and slipped into a seat. He was half in the chair and half out of it, as one might sit at the edge of a buckboard, resting one foot on the step. In this alert position he waited for food.

When it came he attacked it with calm and patient energy. Eggs, bacon, flapjacks beyond number, an immense glass of milk, flowed into the insatiable pit of Bud. At length he slipped back in his chair and regarded his host.

"Pretty good feed," he said to the sheriff. "Thanks!"

They were enjoying cigarettes. Mr. Aiken permitted himself to smile at the appetite of Bud. The priest was too wise to do so; the sheriff would never have dreamed of it.

"My servant, Joe," he said, "tells me that you was around late last night trying to see me."

"I dunno. Why, yes," drawled Bud, "I may of dropped around that way."

The sheriff was instantly full of interest. He knew the meaning of Bud's nonchalance, as a rule.

"By the way," he said, "I guess you know you was right. Lucky showed up at Mat's place, right enough."

"Did he?" yawned Bud. "Then I guess you grabbed him—or potted him, most like."

"We could have done it," groaned Aiken. "When he

189

first came up to Mat's shack, every one of us had a bead drawn on him, and we could have sent him to hell a dozen ways. Asking your pardon, Father Connell.''

The priest raised a hand in a gesture which conveyed both rebuke and pardon. He was watching Bud.

"I met a gent on the road yesterday," said Bud. "He was quite some gent, too. Handiest I ever see with a gun—leaving you out, sheriff."

He conveyed this generous compliment to the sheriff with a courtly wave of his brown hand.

"Thanks," said Jud Nevil.

"Him and me had quite a talk," went on the boy. "I gathered that he would of gone partnerships in catching Lucky—if I'd throwed in with him."

"Split the coin fifty-fifty with you?" asked the sheriff.

"Something like that, saying I'd brought him where Lucky was. We didn't make no dicker, but he was one of the kind that you don't need to talk everything over with."

"If you brought him to Lucky Bill?" asked the sheriff. "You mean, to Mat's house?"

"Mat Morgan's house?" echoed the boy with scorn. "No, that was *your* game, Sheriff."

"Sure, and I made a mess of it."

"Better luck next time," said the boy with much grace.

"Thanks."

The priest, all this time, had been looking Bud narrowly in the eye.

"My friend," he now said, "I think you have something to tell us. Something important."

"I dunno," remarked Bud, shrugging his shoulders.

"We're listening."

"All depends on how you look at it," said Bud philosophically. "Maybe you and Mr. Aiken are kind of interested in finding Miss Aiken?"

"Kind of," admitted the priest with a good-natured smile.

"Well, she's at old Taliaferro's house."

There was a cry from the men at the table.

"When did you find this out?" asked Aiken, excited.

"Last night."

"You infernal little whelp—and you didn't tell us?"

The cold eye of Bud went over the rancher from head to foot.

"I dropped around to the sheriff's place," he said; "but he couldn't see me. He was busy sleeping."

There was a groan from them all.

"Mostly," he said, "I thought the sheriff would like to know where Lucky Bill is."

"Well?" breathed Nevil.

"I reckon he's in the same place."

"Boy," cried Mr. Aiken, "your home is with me from now on."

"Speaking of homes," declared Bud coldly, "we all got our own ideas. A rat likes a hole and a buzzard likes a tree."

But this mysterious remark received scant attention. The sheriff was already issuing orders. And in a few minutes the preparation of the posse was already under way. It was no easy thing to manage. Those who had ridden so far and watched so long the day before were by no means willing to undertake another expedition. The sheriff had to comb over a new list of possibilities. Bud interrupted him.

"This time," he said, "maybe you'll let me go along—just for luck, Sheriff?"

"Son, is that still on your mind? Nope. You ain't old enough, Bud, nor big enough. I ain't going to have you on my conscience. You run along."

"And yet," said Bud bitterly, as he found his way back to Pinto, "he's taking along a priest that ain't no kind of a fighting man. But this show I'm going to see."

While the sheriff was still busy gathering his men, Bud slipped upon Pinto and started out for the far-off Taliaferro house.

Chapter Twenty-one

Diplomacy

There was light sleep for Lucky Bill that night in the Taliaferro house. Twice during the evening he had attempted to bring the old man back to the subject of the girl, but it seemed the host felt he had already said enough, and each time he dexterously turned the talk to other things.

At last Lucky gave up in despair, and going out to the shed, since there was no bed in the house for him, he curled up in the hay and tried to rest.

Even when sleep came his dreams stayed with him and disturbed his rest, so that when he wakened in the morning he felt as if he had aged greatly during the night. For one thing, it seemed to him that he had known Molly Aiken half his life.

First of all, he wondered how she would meet him at

breakfast. His doubts were quickly put at rest. She met him as if nothing unusual had happened recently within her ken. Lucky found himself much constrained, and his eyes uneasily roved around the table. Or sometimes he cast covert glances at her; but she was always at ease.

She seemed to find old Taliaferro himself far more entertaining and worthy of talk. She seemed different from the Molly Aiken of the day before, only in that she was excited by little things. The cooking of George called forth extravagant praise that set the old negro grinning with delight. And opening the shade at the end of the room, she declared that the sun had never been so bright. Or when Mr. Taliaferro ventured a jest which was stale enough to Lucky, the girl burst into peals of delicious merriment.

On each of these occasions the old man looked to Lucky and nodded wisely, as though it were something for Lucky to understand and smile at covertly. But the big man was entirely bewildered. It seemed absurd for Taliaferro to connect these outbursts of extravagance with any feeling she had for him. He was angered by the hints which his host's eyes conveyed.

In truth, Lucky was wretchedly in love. When the girl spoke, his heart jumped. When he looked at her his eyes grew misty. And somewhere in the pit of his stomach there was a peculiar and empty ache.

After breakfast she did not even stay to talk to him, but ran out for a walk. It left Lucky downheaded. Mr. Taliaferro came to him and spoke sternly; every word had a cruel point.

"You dunderheaded idiot!" was his opening. "Are you blind? Go out there and find her!"

"I got an idea," said Lucky, with an attempt at dignity, "that she'd rather be alone. She didn't say nothing about wanting company."

"Company your foot!" snorted the old man. "Will you do what I tell you to do?"

Lucky was strangely humble.

"What is it?" he said.

"Go out and tell her you love her. And do it now!"

He fairly thrust Lucky out of the house, and the big man, having settled his hat firmly over his eyes, strode off after the girl. He made a brave appearance; but his heart was like water.

He found her prying into the depths of an old combination barn and granary. The great mow was empty of hay; above was the floor of what had been the granary, and there was still a strong running rod and tackle with which the sacks had been hoisted to the top of the building, and from this point of vantage the grain had been fed, as it was needed, through shoots to the lower part of the barn. It was best in repair of all the buildings on the old ranch, and though the roof sagged in the center, and the walls drooped inward in a knock-kneed fashion, the barn was still an imposing structure.

She was apparently full of her discoveries when he found her. "You could put a hundred horses in this barn, I guess," she said. "And it'll stand up another ten years, anyway."

"I thought," said Lucky with inexcusable bluntness, "that maybe you'd want to know what happened yesterday. But I guess Taliaferro told you."

"Not a word. I couldn't drag a syllable out of him," confessed Molly Aiken. "And of course I want to know."

She sat down on the lid of a feed box, dusty, and

polished by long handling. Lucky stood before her. All at once it seemed that yesterday had been nothing; nothing worth making into a set story, at least.

"Well," he said, "I just went to Mat and told him you'd sort of—" He paused for a word.

"Poor Mat!" cried the girl. "How is his arm now?" It shook Lucky.

"Anyway," he said in sudden confusion, "I got there, and saw Mat, and about a dozen gents under Sheriff Nevil tried to jump me."

"Sheriff Nevil!"

"They've got a price on my head, you see?"

"The cowards! Oh, Lucky!"

All at once he was convinced that Taliaferro was a wise man. For her eyes were at once both bright and misty, and she had made a peculiar cherishing gesture, as though those small hands could keep him from harm. Lucky became dizzy with happiness.

"It ain't nothing," he declared. "It'll be a long time before they collect that five thousand on me. Anyway, I slipped away through the window and got clean out. They run me back into the trees, and then I broke through 'em again. Had a pile of luck."

"Through the window—into the trees—broke through them again! Lucky, what has happened? What have you done? How many—"

"I didn't touch a man," he said. "And I ain't going to again in a hurry." He grinned at the memory. "I met up with a kid that showed me myself in a mirror, and what I saw wasn't pretty to look at. He was better'n a preacher."

"But you got away. They didn't hurt you?"

"Me? Sure they didn't. The burning of the house rattled them."

"Burning house! Lucky, tell me this instant exactly how everything happened!"

"Well, I saw Mat. Told him you'd changed your mind, and——"

"Did I tell you to tell him that?"

"What else could I say?" he asked, amazed by her anger. "Wasn't that what you said?"

"I suppose you couldn't have been diplomatic. Go on, please!"

She seemed to have lost all interest in his story.

He continued perfunctorily: "Then Mat wanted me to bring you to him; then he wanted me to tell him where you were. I held off and told him I'd take him where you were."

"You told him that, in spite of the fact that I'd—"

Then she added fiercely: "Go on!"

"But it seemed like Mat wasn't too ready to start for you. He made a funny play. I called it; I seen he was trying to double cross me, smashed the lamp at his feet; jumped through the window, rode into the woods—they headed me back with their rifle shots; and then busted out past the house and got clean away. That's all!"

He stopped, mopping his forehead.

Words had formed silently on her lips several times during this recital; once she had drawn in a deep breath. But now that he ended she said not a syllable of praise or blame. She sat for a long time looking into the distance. Lucky wished he could know her thoughts just then.

"He wanted you to bring me to him? I'm glad, Lucky Bill—I'm glad you were enough of a gentleman to refuse that. But would you have brought him to me?''

"I've told you I would."

"In spite of—"

"I'd given him my word, and—"

"But your word was to bring *me* to *him*."

"I didn't dare to face you again. I told him that."

"Ah!"

He could not exactly interpret that exclamation. It might have meant almost anything.

"And why not? Why didn't you dare?"

"Because, if I met you again, like that, I'd have to tell you—that I love you, Molly."

He discovered that she was neither pale nor red. She was interweaving her fingers and drawing them apart again, and she studied him from beneath puckered brows as though she could hardly understand what he said.

"Understand," he explained heavily, "I ain't asking that you care a rap about me. But I had to be honest. I wouldn't of dreamed of saying a word. But when I found out that Mat Morgan was a skunk—"

She stopped him by stamping on the floor.

"That's an ugly word!" she cried at him. "Mat Morgan—at least he was *once* my friend."

"An ugly word is the only kind that fits him," declared Lucky, and he frowned in turn.

"Delicacy might have taught you something better."

"Delicacy," said the big man savagely, "kept me from filling him full of lead; and delicacy had a darned hard job to do that much. Far as words go, I could say things about him a lady wouldn't like to hear."

"You might have thought of that before, you know."

"My first thought was tolerably good," said Lucky hotly.

"I wish to return to the house," said the girl.

She was standing rigid, her lips colorless and compressed.

"I guess I ain't blocking your way none," said Lucky, folding his arms.

At that she cast a sidewise glance at him.

"You're just a bully!" breathed Molly Aiken, and fled past him.

When he had recovered from the shock, he followed at a more leisurely pace. At the door he smashed his knuckles into the boards and knocked a long length of rotting plank out of it. Then he strode on to the house.

One great wish occupied his mind—that old Taliaferro were fifty years younger and three inches taller. When he found his host in the house he sneered: "As a mind reader you're a good hoss breaker, Mr. Taliaferro, and as a hoss breaker I wouldn't bet no money on you."

To his surprise the fiery little old man took no offense. He even seemed amused.

"I see," he said, "that you've made a mess of things. What did you say to her?"

"I dunno," growled Lucky, "and damned if I care. She ain't no ways reasonable."

"You hurt her feelings, my boy."

"Feelings? She ain't got none! All I done was say that Mat Morgan was a skunk, and she got all riled."

"My heavens, boy, wasn't that the man she thought she was in love with?"

"I dunno. I suppose so."

"And you called him a skunk to her face?"

"It ain't the half of what he is," cried Lucky. "He's a—"

There followed a minute description of the ancestry

of Mat Morgan, a prophecy as to his probable future, and an eloquently expressed prayer that he would soon recover the use of his injured arm so that he, Lucky, could have the exquisite pleasure of tearing him limb from limb.

He was heard patiently to the end.

Then: "You go off and cool down. After a while, you come back and I'll give you one more piece of advice."

Lucky obeyed. But he found that next piece of advice was hard to win. He came back sullenly at first, and asked for the new suggestion with a sneer; but before evening he was biting his lips with anxiety.

"Has she said anything?" he pleaded of Taliaferro. "Has she told you what a low-down hound I am?"

"D'you think you're as bad as all that?" queried the old man.

"I dunno. I guess I am, partner. I should of known I was hurting her feelings. But I got sort of blind while I was talking to her. Mr. Taliaferro, maybe I'd ought to go and ask her to forgive me for what I said?"

But old Taliaferro struck his hands together.

"Where did you learn about women?" he demanded. "Son, get on your horse and ride to the nearest town. Which is nearest?"

"Waterton, I suppose."

"It's getting dark now, but that don't make any difference. Climb on your hoss and ride to Waterton. You can get back before morning."

"But what for?"

"For a marriage license!" said this surprising octogenarian.

Chapter Twenty-two

New Names

Bud approached the house of Taliaferro for the second
time with a feeling of finality. Once before he had
guessed the course of Lucky Bill, and brought him near
to ruin in the shack of Mat Morgan. He was singularly
sure now that the end had come for the outlaw.

If he felt an exultation it was rather in the foretaste
of the confusion of the stern men of Wheeler when they
should be forced to admit that a boy had outguessed their
fighting men; and surely that affair would give him his
diploma and rank him definitely among the grown-ups.

Yet his heart fell as he came again into the environs
of the old ranch house. He had far rather that the sheriff
had formed his posse more quickly and that they had all
come together. This work as an advance guard was not
at all to his taste. Moreover, the time was worse than

moonlit night. The evening had passed the moment of color. The sky had gone gray, and, though there was still a pale rising light to the west, the earth was already black.

It was that most solemn time of quiet just before the coming of deep night. Bud, in his place of espionage, saw all things slowly changing. He thought that a lamp had been lighted inside the house, and then he discovered that it was only the gleam of the last sunset light across the windowpane.

There was not a sound in the house. What made this the more mysterious was that he knew the girl to be there, and probably Lucky Bill with her, to say nothing of old Taliaferro himself. The latter might live without sound, but the boy connected Lucky Bill with shouts and singing.

Then—it happened with a disconcerting suddenness—a door opened, slammed with a violence that sent an echo among the barns, and a big man ran down from the back veranda. In that dim light he seemed gigantic, the more so because Bud was crouched close to the earth, looking up. The man went past him with monstrous steps that were like leaps.

His face was black with the evening, as though he had worn a mask, and the hand of Bud turned to ice as he gripped the butt of his revolver. It would be the easiest shot he had ever tried, but somehow it was impossible to fire. Yet he knew it was Lucky. He was perfectly certain. The crunch of those heavy footsteps was alone enough to convince him.

When the huge fellow had swept past him it seemed to Bud that about the swing of the broad shoulders there was something familiar—something at once new and old, like the appearance of a well-known house at night. Then the man disappeared into the night.

There were noises in a shed, the unmistakable *flop* as a saddle was flung on the back of a horse, and the grunt of protest from the animal. Another faint groan as the mustang complained under the pull of the cinch. And now a door was opened on creaking hinges, and the steps of a horse sounded, coming into the open. Was it possible that Lucky had received a warning and was about to flee?

It sent Bud trembling to the side of Pinto—trembling with rage because the quarry was about to escape, and with terror because he knew that he must pursue the fugitive. There was a burst of heavy hoofbeats as the horse broke into a gallop, and Bud, groaning faintly through his set teeth, swung onto the back of Pinto.

It was shame that drove him. He had failed of courage when the big man raced past him in the night. And now he was determined to wipe out that disgrace by following the outlaw and bringing him to bay. Cautiously, for fear Pinto might step on some of the deadwood around the buildings and make an alarming crackle, he wove through the outhouses and came into the open in time to see the fugitive loom for an instant on the top of a distant hill against the horizon and then plunge into the blackness beyond.

Bud touched Pinto with his heels and darted off like a bird in pursuit. He was confident of keeping in touch with the other. The finest horse that stepped in the mountain desert could not keep away from Pinto—not with the handicap of the cowpuncher's saddle and the weight of a grown man to burden it. So Bud rode with confidence, and yet with caution. For he could never tell when the ear of the other might catch the sound of his own horse pursuing and draw aside to hunt the hunter.

What he wanted to do was to keep in touch with the outlaw from a distance until an opening came for closing on the man and shooting him down. Perhaps he would draw rein at the top of a hill in clear view and afford a perfect target even in the night light. There were a score of possibilities, and the heart of Bud beat high with hope. No rules of fair play need trouble him. An outlaw was on a par with a beast of the fields. He was a wolf, a coyote, to be shot down from ambush and a price collected for his head.

He found it easy to accomplish his purpose. The outlaw was not riding at top speed, at least after the first burst of running. He had rated his horse to a steady lope, and Pinto followed with never a hard-drawn breath. His sharp little ears were pricked forward, and his head tossed up and down, blotting out the form of the pursued and bringing him into view again. Perhaps it would be a long trail.

Then Bud, taking note of their direction, became worried. As far as he could make out, the trail they followed led nowhere except to the village of Waterton, and desperate though Lucky Bill might be, he would certainly not be fool enough to put his head in the mouth of the lion. Yet as the miles spun out there was little question that this was the goal of the outlaw. He even broke out of the hills and descended into the well-beaten trail, and Bud followed, his wonder growing at every moment.

It was not possible; he could hardly believe his eyes when the fugitive drew rein on top of the hill overlooking the village, and then, as though summoning his resolution, dipped straight down upon the town. Bud followed at a greater distance than before. Two things now opened before him. He could rouse a few men in the town and take Lucky in a net, or he could himself press up on the outlaw and make a gunplay of his own.

The latter was the great temptation. At one stroke to lift himself out of boyhood into manhood. After that, what would the sheriff say when he asked to be included in a manhunt? No, he would not have to ask; he would be the first invited. He heard in foretaste the rumor which swept over the mountain desert, carrying his name to every distant village as the conqueror of Lucky Bill. With this determination making his heart beat wildly, he pushed Pinto harder and began to gain rapidly on the outlaw's horse.

Coming to the outskirts of the village, Lucky brought back his horse to a trot. Because he could run fast enough to keep in touch and because the sound of his trotting horse would be sure to be heard by the outlaw when they entered the street of the town, Bud dismounted, cached Pinto behind a shed with the rope thrown over his head, and raced on into the single street of Waterton.

He was in time to see the rider stop a man in a buckboard, one leaving late for some adjoining ranch house, and hold a short parley with the latter. After which Lucky used the spurs and shot the mustang ahead at full speed, the hoofbeats muffled by the thick dust. And Bud followed as fast as he could run, skulking close to the fronts of the shacks and deep in their shadow.

He darted past the man in the buckboard, who was starting his pair of horses on and beginning a drunken song. He shot around a curve of the street, and saw that Lucky Bill had actually stopped and dismounted before a house, on the door of which he was beating heavily with his fist.

Might it not be the house of some confederate? Was there not a chance, here, to unveil the criminal connections of the outlaw? The possibilities swarmed into the head of Bud until he was dizzy. He was filled with a deathly fear, and at the same time his brain was singing with exultation. He was afraid of only one thing—that in the crisis his hand would be trembling so much that he dared not use his revolver. And yet something told him that in the pinch his nerves would be like steel.

Stealing more cautiously across the intervening distance, he heard someone awaken and come grumbling to the door. He saw that door opened, and a man stood in the entrance with a lamp in his hand. He was dressed in undershirt and trousers, one suspender over his shoulder and the other dangling, a pot-bellied little man with a fierce array of whiskers. Bud was instantly convinced that he had indeed unearthed a silent partner of the outlaw.

But now Lucky entered the house and the door closed. Down the side of the house Bud saw the light flash in window after window and come to a pause in the rear, burning steadily.

Toward this shaft of light he crept, fearful of every noise, even of his own breathing. He had the revolver out and in his hand. Deftly he tried the action of the gun. It worked with silken lightness and smoothness.

He tried the veranda with his hand, and then with his foot. It did not creak. Now he was on it, and, crouched at the open window, he beheld the little fat man at work writing upon a piece of paper. The outlaw stood with his hand dropped loosely on his hips, and something about the back view—the big shoulders with the cleft between the shoulder blades—made Bud start violently.

Unavoidably he made a noise, and at this the outlaw whirled. And then Bud saw. It was the man of the trail, the big man, the kindly hero who had showed him how to "squeeze" a gun, and had wished him luck in the pursuit of Lucky Bill.

Bud sank down against the wall beneath the window with every ounce of physical and moral strength sapped from his muscles.

Chapter Twenty-three

The Partners

Heavy, swift footsteps, approaching the window, walked up against his very ear. Someone was standing above him. He had expected that a great hand would settle around his neck and drag him up into the light like a drowned rat. He hardly cared. In a desperate wave of self-disgust Bud remembered how he had planned to shoot this man from ambush like a wild animal.

Other things came to him—the peculiar fervor with which the big man had pleaded the case of Lucky Bill— and the humility with which he had accepted the judgments of Bud. To have hounded such a man—to have drawn the sheriff on the trail of his very hero! In a burst of shame and grief Bud swore that the little finger of Lucky was worth more than the sheriff and his entire posse.

"Thought I heard a noise out here," said the familiar voice.

"My old Maltese cat. She's snooping around, most like."

"Most like," responded Lucky.

Bud sighed with relief when the footsteps retreated to the center of the room again. He raised his head with care and looked in once more upon the scene.

"And the name of the girl?" asked the fat man, brushing his whiskers with a stubby thumb and forefinger.

"Molly—no, Martha Aiken, it is. Molly's the nickname, I guess."

The little man paused, with his pen poised, and then wrote again on the paper. Presently he detached this from the pad and shoved it across the desk.

"There you are. Kind of in a hurry with this marriage, ain't you?"

"Sorry I got you up, but we had to rush it through, and we couldn't do without a marriage license, you see."

"Sure. Wait a minute; I'll blot that." The fat man opened a drawer of the desk, but Lucky had already picked up the little sheet of paper. He was holding it in both hands, blowing on it to dry the ink.

"Never mind, partner—this'll do. Now what's the damages? I'd like to—"

Bud saw the little fat man straighten, and his hand whipped up out of the drawer bearing a long, blue-bright revolver. He held it with both hands, leveling it across the top of his desk.

"Lucky Bill!" he snapped. "Get up them hands!"

To have attempted a gunplay, even for Lucky Bill,

would have been pure madness. The muzzle of that revolver was not six feet away, and it was gripped in one of the clerk's hands, while the other steadied the barrel and made a rifle out of the weapon. Lucky pushed his hands slowly up above his head.

"You may be tolerable bright, partner," he said—and Bud admired from the deeps of his heart the steadiness of that voice—"but who put this fool idea into your head?"

At this the little man puckered his mouth with satisfaction, so that the whiskers bulged out on either side of his face.

"You can't talk me out of it," he declared. "I know you. I've seen the posters that Nevil got out. But what let me in on it was the name of the girl. We all know you run away with Molly Aiken, Lucky. You sure was a fool to come into town and try to get away with this. Hey, keep that right hand above the line of your ear, friend, or I'll just naturally blow you plumb to hell. I mean business!"

Lucky obeyed.

"You might do things like this in Wheeler," continued the other, "but Waterton's different. We ain't asleep like Wheeler is."

"Well," said Lucky genially, "this is a nice, fat haul for you. But it's a big laugh if you're wrong. I guess the folks will never get done giving you the laugh when they hear how you held me up and thought I was Lucky Bill!" And he even laughed himself.

It staggered even Bud for the moment, and the fat man allowed his eyes to widen. But he clung to his gun and scowled to restore his nerve.

"I guess I'll see this through," he said. "You tally

pretty close with the description of Bill. Just back up agin' that wall and turn your back to me, Bill.''

''Wait a minute, fatty,'' said Bud.

There was a convulsive start from the fat man. But he dared not for the least fraction of an instant divert his glance from Lucky Bill. The split part of a second would suffice for the gunfighter to whip a hand down to a weapon and make a play with it. The fat man turned pale.

''Wait a minute, fatty,'' said Bud, beginning to enjoy the scene. ''I'm right outside the window here. I got my gat lying on the edge of the sill, and I got a bead laid right between your eyes. I can almost hardly keep my finger off'n the trigger, it's such a pretty shot!''

The fat hero moaned.

''Just cast an eye over here, and you'll see the muzzle of my gun. Now, the best move for you is take up that great big gun of yours and put it back in the drawer, and then stand up and put your hands over your head and turn your back on my friend in there. And do all them things tolerable slow. Because I got an awful itchy finger on this trigger, as I was saying a while back, and if you was to move sudden I might send a slug through the window—see?''

The other was a trembling wreck of a man. Even his fat paunch quivered. And he obeyed to the letter. With marvelous softness he took the gun from the top of the desk and deposited it in the drawer. Then he rose, moving as slowly as a sleepwalker, cast a desperate glance at the smiling face of Lucky, and then twitched around so that his back was to the outlaw. ''Partner,'' he whined, ''you don't bear no malice because—''

''Not a bit,'' said Lucky. ''I'm just going to tie you

and gag you, so's you won't make no noise for a time. I guess that's fair.''

In a trice he had firmly secured the other and worked a strong gag between his teeth. He left him lying on the floor, his eyes bulging and his cheeks purple. His face was like that of some great fish drawn out of water and now at the last gasp.

With this, Lucky went to the window, jerked it open, and stood face-to-face with Bud.

''You!'' he said at length, and dropped a heavy hand on the shoulder of the boy.

''Me,'' sighed Bud, trembling he knew not why.

That was all. The outlaw strode off down the porch, and Bud followed him. And when Lucky swung into his saddle, Bud trudged down the street on foot beside him until they reached the shed at the end of the village, and there he resumed his place on the back of Pinto, and the two swung in side by side on the back trail. One might have thought that they had long been partners of the ranges.

''Of all the pinches I ever been in,'' said the outlaw at length, ''that was the tightest. I was done for; then I heard you speak up.''

To the end of his life Bud was never to know a pleasure so great as this simple statement of fact. But where was the sheriff and his posse by this time?

Lucky had broke into a soft laughter.

''And to think that you knew me all the time when I met you the other day! Partner—what's your name?''

''Bud.''

''Well, Bud, I been thinking a good deal about that little lecture that you read me. It done me a pile more good than any preacher I ever heard. And you knowing me all the time and pretending you was on the trail of Lucky Bill. Bud, you sure got a sense of humor. And I don't mind if you tell the yarn on me. I can stand being laughed at by gents like you."

Something swelled in the throat of Bud. Presently he said, "You're going to marry that girl, Lucky?"

"Sure, if I can. I'm taking a pot shot for luck."

"Here's hoping you have it," said Bud. "Speaking of girls, Lucky, I guess it's mostly chance, anyway."

He saw the other turn his head in the darkness, and guessed that there was a smile on the unseen face.

"But how'd you happen to stumble on me in that house?" asked Lucky.

Bud stumbled miserably into the truth. "Lucky, I got to tell you: When I met you on the road I wasn't joking. I didn't know you was Lucky Bill. I was on your trail."

"D'you mean that? Well, they's still a laugh in it."

"But wait! You'll sure hate me before I get through. I thought Lucky Bill was plumb bad, you see. Girl stealer and all that, like they said you was. So I figured out where you'd most likely be hiding. I guessed the haunted house of old Taliaferro. So I went there and snooped around till I seen the girl. Then I knowed you'd be there, too. So I went back to Wheeler. Lucky, will you ever forgive me?"

"Go on, partner. I'd forgive you a heap. What'd you do in Wheeler?"

"I—I told the sheriff where you was hanging out."

There was neither a groan nor a curse, but a breath of silence more eloquent to Bud than any denunciation.

"He's coming there tonight," continued Bud, feeling the ashes of shame and sorrow falling on his heart. "And—Lucky, I'd give an arm to help."

He waited. At length there came a strained voice which said: "Partner, when a gent has done for me what you've done, he don't have to do no explaining."

"But what you going to do?" asked Bud, biting his lip to keep it from trembling.

"I'm going back to Taliaferro's."

"In spite of the sheriff?"

"In spite of ten like him!"

"Then I'm with you, Lucky."

And they spurred their horses forward at the same moment.

Chapter Twenty-four

Molly's Role

"It must be Marse Lucky come back," said George, when the knock came at the door.

"He's not the kind that turns back," said old Taliaferro, frowning.

Molly Aiken stood up with a changed face.

"Is there trouble?" she whispered. "Is there trouble about Lucky? Do you thinks it's someone else?"

"It's just Marse Lucky. He's forgot something and come back," persisted George, shaking his head.

"You old fool," said the master sternly. "Lucky isn't the kind that forgets things. He's gone; this is someone else."

"I'll find out, sir."

"We'll find out together."

They went toward the door, and the girl made up a trembling rear to the party.

The front door quivered under the third knock.

"Who's there?" asked George.

"Open!" cried the voice of a stranger.

"Is that Lucky's voice?" sneered old Taliaferro to the negro. He stepped forward. "Who's there?"

"An officer of the law. Open in the name of the law!"

There was an awful ring in that voice; it seemed that the old house was suddenly beleaguered by inescapable forces.

"There's no need of the law here," boomed old Taliaferro in his great voice. "Pass on."

"Break the door, Sheriff," called another from without.

"It's Dad," gasped Molly Aiken.

Mr. Taliaferro ground his teeth and drew himself to his full height. He cast one glance of rage toward the door as if he yearned to fling himself upon it, tear it open, and scatter the men without like dead leaves before the whirlwind. Then, realizing that he was no longer what he had once been, he called: "Gentlemen, wait a moment until I can bring the key."

"All right. Make it pronto. Jerry—Grundy—take the back of the house and look sharp."

"And don't waste time asking questions. Shoot on sight!" called the voice of Aiken.

Taliaferro blocked the path of the girl as she turned to flee.

"Now what's in your mind, Miss Aiken?" he asked bluntly.

"I'm going to get away!"

"With those fools shooting on sight?"

Gun Gentlemen

"I've got to get away! Dad—"

"Is he worse than a .45-caliber bullet?"

"I'd rather die than have him catch me! I'd a thousand times rather die!"

"Madam," said the old man, "the law is often blind and usually stupid, but as a rule it has its way. Those men are coming through that door, in about a minute. Now make up your mind as to what you're going to do."

"There's no escape? There must be a way!"

"If I were ten years younger," he said through his teeth, "I'd—but I'm not. I'm old, tottering. I'm no help with my hands. Now, what are you going to do?"

"If he enters this house by force, knowing I'm here, he ceases to be my father—he's a stranger to me."

"You're going to let him know that?"

"I'll tell him that much—and then never open my lips to him so long as I live."

A faint smile flickered over the face of the octogenarian. He nodded.

"I understand, but it won't do. Your father, I take it, is full of your own blood."

"He can be outrageous!"

"I don't doubt it. And when you denounce him and then refuse to speak, he'll put you in close confinement and keep you guarded—maybe for a year at a stretch."

"Is this country free? Have I no rights?"

"Very few," smiled Taliaferro. "Not where your father is concerned. But our point is this: You wish to have as much liberty as possible, eh?"

"Of course."

"So that you may have a chance to get away and find Lucky and warn him about what has happened here?"

"Lucky—is a boor. I hope I never——"

"Hush! You wish him to fall into the trap? To return while the sheriff is here and be caught?"

"Oh," cried the girl, "I wish that I'd never been born!"

"You can rest assured," he went on rapidly, raising his voice a little, because there was a steady clamor at the door, and someone was shaking it violently to try the lock. "You can rest assured that if you do not go to him, Lucky will come to you. I know his mind and his temper. He'll risk ten posses for you. You can only forestall him by going to him."

"I would," she stammered, wringing her hands. "But how can I escape?"

"By making them think that you hate the ground Lucky walks. Quick! I've only a moment to make you understand. They're smashing the door, the curs! Tell your father that Lucky carried you off by brute force— that you detest him. Pretend he is saving you from—"

The door went in with a crash, and the two men who had beaten it down by lunging their weight against it, toppled into the dusty hall and sprawled. In the doorway behind them stood a pack of men with weapons in their hands. They entered on the run, scattering according to the shrill commands of the sheriff. Some he sent toward the stairs to search the upper part of the house. He directed that four men remain outside to watch the corners of the house.

And out of the swirl of running men came Henry Aiken, a heavy-shouldered man with iron-gray hair and iron in his face as he caught sight of his daughter. Old Taliaferro cast one glance at him and then turned a gaze of anxiety upon Molly. She hesitated for one instant, with a glimmer of rage in her eyes, and then ran with a cry and threw herself into the arms of her father.

His face made such a study in comic strife of emotions that old Taliaferro gritted his teeth to keep from laughter. When she ran toward him, he had braced himself as though to meet the charge of a fighting man, and now that he held her in his arms, fury, bewilderment, relief, in rapid succession, swept over his face.

He carried on a harsh monologue at the same time, which Taliaferro followed somewhat in this manner: "So I have you, eh? And, young lady, I'll teach you that I know how to keep you! Branded, that's what we should do with our girls; brand 'em so that other men can know the ownership! Thank God your mother is dead! You'd be the death of her otherwise! Confound it, Molly, stop crying. Your whims have turned my hair white in a day. Molly, dear, it's all right; I'm here to take care of you!"

So he had passed in one moment from rage to the business of quieting her. She was sobbing—real tears of excitement and anger, as Taliaferro knew. Finally her father pushed her away.

"Molly," he demanded, "did you run away because you were fond of the skunk, or simply to spite me?"

"I don't know," said Molly.

"You don't know?" roared Aiken.

"Oh, Dad, I'll never stop being grateful that you found me!"

"H'm!" he growled, pacified again. "You need your dad still, eh? Old man ain't quite useless yet?"

"I couldn't help it; he took me away by force!"

"I'll have his hide! The dog! But what were you doing waiting out there, eh? Answer me that?"

"I was waiting to tell him I'd changed my mind."

"And he took you, anyway? Oh, he'll pay for it! The yellow-hearted cur!"

"He's not a cur!" cried Molly.

"What? He's not?"

She stamped her foot. "No, no, no!"

Taliaferro stepped between them.

"And who the devil are you?" shouted Aiken.

"Mr. Aiken, don't you see that your girl is hysterical?"

She took the cue and burst into a rage of tears, and Taliaferro took her in his arms.

"I hate him!" she whispered in his ear. "And I'll throw the words in his face if he says that about Lucky again!"

"What's that?" thundered Aiken.

"She's asked me to explain," said Taliaferro. "I'll do my best. It's a tangled affair, sir; but I think I can make heads and tails of it. She's had a hard time; be easy with her, Mr. Aiken."

"Bless us!" growled the rancher. "She deserves a hard time. It comes from playing fast and loose—"

"It's not true," stormed Molly, breaking away from Taliaferro. "And he's—"

"Hush!" said an authoritative voice, not loud, but remarkably dominant. "Molly, be quiet. Mr. Aiken, not another word. My dear, come to me and tell me about all this."

And Father Connell stepped between them. Aiken had started forward, but the solemnly raised hand of the priest stopped him.

"I'll have the truth down to the last scruple," shouted the rancher. "Or by the Lord she'll live in a dark room on bread and water till she tells me!''

"Sir!'' exclaimed Father Connell, and to Molly: "We'll sit down together, my dear, and talk it smooth.''

"This way,'' said Taliaferro, and he led them into his sanctum. There he detained the rancher and kept him in talk at one end of the room.

"A terrible affair,'' said Taliaferro. "My home invaded by a desperado; this poor girl foisted onto my hands; and all I could do was to keep her from him. A terrible man, Mr. Aiken.''

"I'll 'terrible' him,'' exclaimed the rancher. "I'll have his heart out for this!''

"You young men,'' said the adroit old Taliaferro, "are able to do such things, but I, you see, am limited by years.''

In the meantime Molly was saying to the priest in a rapid whisper. "It's all a lie. He didn't murder Harry. It was a fair fight; and the death was an accident. And—and—I love him, Father Connell, and I ll never rest till I find him again!''

"If you love him, my dear,'' said the quiet priest, "this is not a matter for worry. It is in the hands of God, and He will bring all to a good end.''

"But Dad mustn't know! If he thought—''

"He shall not know. Not for a time. In the meantime, the man is outlawed. Is it not better for us all to go quietly home and wait?''

"Father Connell, I can't wait! Don't you know that?''

"I'm afraid I do, my dear Molly.''

"And you shall help me!''

"I'm afraid I shall,'' said the wise priest, and he smiled at her.

Things were at a pause; there was nothing to be done

221

but figure the trail of the fugitive by guesswork and then start on; but the sheriff was slow in admitting that the trap had failed to catch the main prize.

At this juncture old George found Mr. Taliaferro and informed him that a young stranger wished to speak to him. He went into the hall and there he found a child with a vast, floppy-brimmed sombrero and a loose man-sized vest, scraping mysterious characters in the dust on the floor with his bare toe.

He viewed the old man attentively with calm eyes.

"Are you the gent that runs this place?" he asked.

"I suppose I am, my young friend."

"You're Taliaferro?"

"I am."

"I'm Bud."

"How do you do, Bud?"

"Pretty well. How's yourself? I got a message for you."

"From whom?"

"Step over here, will you!"

"Very well."

They were in a corner effectually screened from sight or hearing, but still Bud beckoned the old man until he stooped and brought his ear close.

"His name," said Bud, "is William Taliaferro. That mean anything to you?"

It meant so much that Taliaferro stiffened and went back a step as though he had been mortally wounded. The color fled from his face.

"Boy," he said, "who taught you to bring this horrible jest to me?"

"Jest?" said Bud scornfully. "Say, mister, that's

something you wouldn't be saying to the gent that sent me here."

"Describe him," said Jefferson Taliaferro.

He was trembling with a painful eagerness.

"Well, he's about six inches taller'n you are."

"True, true! William was a far larger man!"

"He's got blue eyes."

"Yes!"

"And a pair of big shoulders."

"Yes."

"He's about twenty-five years old—"

There was a groan from old Taliaferro. He caught the boy by the shoulders, his wrinkled old hands closing on the flesh like powerful talons.

"Go easy," protested Bud, shivering under the pain of that clutch, but disdaining to show his uneasiness by trying to break away. "I'm tolerable patient, but I hate to be mauled around. I don't stand handling, you see."

"Go back to the fool who sent you," said Taliaferro, "and tell him that he presumes on my age, but he may presume too far."

"I knew," answered the boy, undaunted and contemptuous, "that nothing would come out of it. But I'll say my say like I was told to say it. And you can lay to this—you're the first gent in the world that ever had the nerve to say that he lied. The rest I was told to say is this: that his name is William Taliaferro, and that his father's name was the same, and that you already know by some token or other that he was wounded at the time that his father was killed. Is that anything to you?"

Taliaferro released his grip upon the shoulders of Bud, and while the boy rubbed the sore places cautiously, making a wry face, Taliaferro leaned against the wall and passed a hand across his face.

"By what name have I known him before?" he whispered hoarsely.

"By a name that ain't none too popular among the thickheads—Lucky Bill."

The eyes of Taliaferro flashed from the floor to the face of the boy and dwelt there with an agonized inquiry. Then they raised.

"God be praised!" he whispered. "From the first moment I guessed it, but I dared not admit it even to myself. It is true!"

"Friend," said the scornful boy, "it's harder to get a lie out of a gent like Lucky Bill than it is to find an apple tree in the desert. You can lay to that."

"There will still be Taliaferros. I am not the end."

"Mr. Taliaferro," said Bud dryly, "according to the gents I've seen around here and the guns they wear, the odds is about ten to one that the Taliaferros ain't going to be any continued story."

"Hush! Hush, child!"

"H-m-m!" muttered Bud, and flushed.

"Where is he?"

"In the big barn behind the house."

"He's mad! The whole posse is here."

"Sure. That's why I got Bill to go there. The last place they'll look for him tonight will be near the house. They'll strike away off, if they ride."

"Why under heaven has he come back?"

"With a marriage license," said Bud calmly.

"I must see him," said Taliaferro eagerly. "William Taliaferro! He has the Taliaferro eye; he has the Taliaferro heart!"

"Later on, a pile later you'll see him," directed Bud.

"If you went out now they'd follow you. What I want to know is this: Are you with us?"

"To the very end. What can I do?"

"These gents have rode quite a lot. Maybe they're tired."

"And hungry," nodded Taliaferro. "I could occupy them by giving them something to eat."

Bud grunted in disgust.

"They ain't a man of 'em that can't go forty-eight hours without chuck," he declared. "But suppose you open up some red-eye for 'em?"

"I have no whisky in the house. I have only some old wine, the very last of my cellar."

"Wine? Well, that might do."

Taliaferro sighed.

"Open up," said Bud. "Start the stuff around. They've missed Lucky. Call 'em in and open up the wine."

Perhaps it would have been easier for Taliaferro to shed his own blood drop by drop than to make this ultimate sacrifice.

"And lemme come in with you; the sheriff thinks I'm on his side."

So old Taliaferro brought Bud back into the library. Mr. Aiken was the first to see him and the first to greet him. He wrung the hands of the boy with tears in his eyes.

"The sheriff himself admits it," he said. "You're the one who has restored Molly to me, Bud. And you can count on my gratitude." He turned to the girl. "Here's the boy who outguessed Lucky Bill, Molly," he said. "And here's the one to whom you owe your thanks."

But Molly was singularly silent and fixed upon Bud such an eye as she might have cast upon a serpent. But the moment which would have made an embarrassing pause was covered by the announcement of Taliaferro that there was drink for the thirsty.

Old George went scurrying down to the cellar and came up with an armful of tall bottles, and the sheriff called in his sentinels. They had done their work; Lucky had slipped through the net. The main thing was to celebrate the recovery of the girl.

Presently there was an odd spectacle in the solemnity of the big library. Dusty cowpunchers lounged around with glasses of fine wine.

"Ain't half bad," pronounced "Rusty John." "Kind of watery, but if you think twice after it goes down, you get a sort of a glow. But why the glasses, governor? Glasses is all right in their place, but the bottle will do for me, Here's to you!"

Seizing a long-throated, pale-green bottle by the nape, he inverted it at his lips, and presently the others heard the bubbling of the liquor as it disappeared. Half a quart emptied at a draft. The sweat stood out on the forehead of Taliaferro. He protested feebly that only in glasses was the taste brought out.

"Damn the taste," chuckled Mr. Aiken. "We want the effect."

And the example of Rusty John was instantly copied around the room. George went down for another armful, and when he returned whispered a gloomy word in the ear of Taliaferro; it was the last of the cellar.

Taliaferro turned pale, but he replied calmly to the old negro: "There are two things which a gentleman should end without undue disturbance: his life and his cellar. Let them drink, George."

Old, old Rhine wine and generous Medoc went tumbling down those thirsty throats. Voices began to open in return. Faces made grim by the hard ride relaxed. Words exploded. Kindly eyes turned upon Taliaferro, who sat very erect, enthroned in his enormous chair. He looked for all the world like some old gentleman pirate celebrating with his ruffian crew the taking of a prize.

From the carnival two people drew back, Father Connell into one corner, and Molly Aiken into the other. Bud approached the girl during the first round of drinks. She met him with a look of deep distaste which made Bud wince.

"Lady," he said heavily, "it ain't hard to see that you'd rather talk to somebody else, but—"

"My father will tell you how grateful I am," said the girl, controlling herself. "In the meantime, I'm very tired. I can't talk to you now. Tomorrow—"

She was surprised to see that a broad grin had spread upon the face of Bud.

"Pretty good," he said critically. "Lucky said you was dead game, but I didn't think a girl could do like this."

One word in his speech amazed her. While she stared he added: "Mostly you're wishing I was about a dozen feet planted under ground."

"Talk softly," said the girl eagerly. "What do you mean?"

"Don't whisper," said he, frowning. "Whispers always make a lot of people look at you. Talk up. They ain't going to hear. Lady, I come from Lucky; he's waiting to see you. Will you go out to the big barn behind the house?"

He added: "Steady! Yawn or something. You look terrible white. They ain't going to be no danger so long as you keep your head. But if you lose your head, everything goes bust.''

"I'll—I'll go—at once,'' said the girl. "Oh, you blessed boy!''

"H-m-m!'' growled Bud, but for the first time in years the term did not irritate him. He even flushed with pleasure.

"You can't just plain up and walk out,'' he said. "They got an eye on you, and they'd follow. You got to take somebody with you.''

"But who could go? I'll take you, Bud!''

"Nope. Not me. But yonder is Father Connell. I got an idea he'd go along. Just tell him that you want to take a look around and a walk, and he'll go. Then you can get him outside the house and out to the barn. Then pop the real reason you went out to him.''

"He'd give an alarm.''

"Lady,'' said the boy solemnly, "he may be a preacher, but he's about nine-tenths man. You try him out.''

Chapter Twenty-five

The Jest

In the very beginning there was a hurdle to top. First
Molly went to Father Connell, and Bud saw the good
priest nod at once and rise, but as they reached the door
of the library, Aiken called after them, excitedly. He had
regained his daughter too recently to risk her out of his
eyes.

She told him, firmly enough, that she and the priest
were out of place at a drinking bout, and that they were
going for a stroll around the house.

"Not in a thousand years," roared Aiken. "You'll
stay here where I can keep a watch on you!"

There was no way of dodging a command like this.
Taliaferro came to the rescue.

"My dear Mr. Aiken," he said, "do you think Lucky
Bill is waiting under the shadow of the house and in

sound of the sheriff's voice to carry off your daughter?''

A roar of laughter came from the posse.

"That reminds me,'' cried the sheriff. And he began a thundering song, which was joined by the others.

Aiken himself was soon beating time and bellowing the chorus, and under cover of this uproar the girl and the priest walked unhindered out of the room.

Bud remained behind them. It was the anxious time for him. And sitting curled up in one of the big chairs near the window, he listened painfully for some sound on the outside. There was no outcry; at least the priest had made no loud objection when he was brought face-to-face with Lucky Bill.

That moment passed. The most difficult part remained. And now Bud stepped to the side of Nevil and touched his arm.

"Sheriff,'' he said—it was in the midst of a song and the sheriff bent his head hastily, still humming, and keeping time with a big bottle in the other hand—"sheriff, I got to say a word to you.''

"Say it, son, pronto!''

"Not in here.''

"Damn it, Bud, what's the secret?''

"It's a joke, sheriff. And I got to have you outside to tell it to you.''

The sheriff sighed, but he owed too much to the boy on this night to refuse his first request. He walked from the room and Bud closed the door behind them. The sheriff looked about him with something of a shiver. And then he frowned at Bud.

"Out with it, son!''

"My joke is farther ahead. You got to come outside the house with me, sheriff.''

"What the devil do you mean by that?"

"Just what I say. Will you come?"

"Tell it to me tomorrow. I'm busy."

But Bud set his shoulders against the door and blocked the way; his jaw was set and his eyes were bright.

"I ask you peaceable," he said.

"Stop this foolishness," growled Nevil.

"Then—" Bud said through his teeth, and jerking his hand from beneath his vest he brought it out bearing the ancient revolver of General Custer. It came with a flash; but it steadied as though it rested on a rock. The sheriff forgot that he had to do with a boy, and he gasped.

"Stick up your hands," said Bud.

The sheriff cursed.

"Pronto!" commanded Bud. "And keep your hands high, too. You hear me talk? The first funny move you make, I'm going to salt you away with lead. That's straight."

"Bud, are you crazy?" pleaded the desperate sheriff, from whose brain the last glow of the wine had departed.

"Nope, but I'm dead set on having you hear that joke I was telling you about. Turn around. March. No, not so fast. And—*keep them hands up*!"

The sheriff could do nothing but obey, and as he trudged forward he felt something small and cold and heavy pressed against his back, and he knew the boy held his life in the curving of his forefinger.

It was a sobering walk for the sheriff. Straight out of the house. When the night air struck his face he paused and cursed softly again.

"Bud," he groaned, "what have you got agin' me?"

"Nothing," said Bud grimly. "I ain't for you and I

ain't agin' you. All I got to say is that if you'd let me
sign up in your posse none of this would be happening.
But you made me play a lone hand. You wouldn't take
me with you. That balances everything. Now, step
along!''

He guided the sheriff brutally by jabbing him with the
muzzle of the revolver. They crossed the backyard; they
reached the yawning blackness which covered the side
entrance to the great ruin of the barn.

"Now," said Bud, "I can't see you. You could make
a quick break, Sheriff, but if you do, I tell you solemn
and true I'll blow you in two!''

"For the Lord's sake, Bud," muttered the sheriff,
"keep your head. I ain't going to make no move!''

"All right. But I ain't trusting you none. Remember
that!''

He called in a guarded voice: "Lucky! It's me—
Bud!''

The sheriff started and drew his breath in sharply
through his teeth with a drinking sound. But he could
not forget the steady pressure of the gun against his
back. Bud called into the darkness: "A friend to see you,
Lucky. Have a light.''

Voices muttered, a match was struck, and to the astonished eyes of the sheriff the tableau was revealed of
Father Connell to one side, his arms folded and his
hands thrust in Chinese fashion into the opposite sleeves;
and near him stood Molly Aiken, while in front was
Lucky holding a match in one hand and a drawn gun in
the other.

The match burned out without a word spoken, and
again there was darkness.

"Are you ready?" asked Bud. "Are you all set, Lucky?"

"For what, partner?"

"For the marriage, I guess."

"What?"

"I don't see nothing missing," said Bud. "Here's the license, the girl, the preacher, and the witness. Need anything more?"

There was a series of muffled exclamations. And Bud heard the girl saying in a voice which he did not recognize. it was so deep and small at once:

"In a church or a barn, what does it matter, Lucky?"

"Father Connell?" said the outlaw. "Did you hear what Bud said?"

"I am here under compulsion, it seems," chuckled the priest, "and I can hardly avoid doing what you ask."

"Lucky Bill," said the sheriff hotly, "you're cool and you're clever—you and the boy—but count me out of this!"

"Sheriff, have you forgot they's a lady here?" said Bud sternly.

"Bud," groaned the sheriff, "don't you see I'm ruined if my name is signed as a witness—on the marriage of a man I'm chasing? What devil put you up to this?"

"It all come out of my own head," said Bud. "Lucky, light another match so's Mr. Connell can begin."

There was the striking of another match. Father Connell was revealed taking a little book out of a pocket of his coat: the girl, bright-eyed. was seen standing at the side of Lucky, looking up at him.

"Look 'em over, Sheriff," said Bud. "Does that gent look like a murderer?"

"Looks is one thing and facts is another. Am I going

to throw up my reputation for a gent like Lucky Bill?''

"Partner," said Bud smoothly, "I've took my gun away from your back. You're free to turn around and beat it if you want to. Lucky won't make no gunplay to get you. You can run out of the barn and get the gents in the house. You're all free to do that, or you can stay here and give Lucky a new start. You seen Molly. D'you think she'd be in love with a gent that wasn't a clean shooter? Here she is ready to climb on a hoss and foller him around the world.''

"She's lost her head," said the sheriff.

"Say that slow," said Bud. "She ain't lost her head. She's found herself out. And you can give them two a pile of happiness and a fine chance, Sheriff. What's there agin' Lucky? That fight with Harry Landrie, and it ain't hard to prove that Landrie was killed by an accident, eh? Well, after the marriage, it's a cinch that old Aiken will take away the reward off the head of Lucky. And then if you get busy and get in touch with the governor, won't he do the same thing? And which would you rather have?

"Would you rather have the gents in Wheeler shaking hands with you because you run down Lucky, or would you rather have Lucky alive and in his boots and a friend of yours, ready to give you a hand if ever some gunfighter started cleaning up Wheeler? I ask you, which would you rather have?

"All you got to do is put down your name as a witness. Then Lucky and Molly ride away and give things a chance to settle down. Inside ten days they'll be back, and they won't be no price on Lucky's head. Then he'll stand a trial for killing Landrie and he'll come out clean. Sheriff, will you do it?''

Darkness had come again; the sheriff was silent.

"I guess you might as well start in, Mr. Connell," said the boy. "I guess the sheriff'll have a chance to think it over while you talk."

In the darkness the priest began the ceremony. Voices answered his questions out of the blackness. Then he lighted a match and Lucky, by that light, took off a ring from his little finger and placed it on the finger of the girl. It was ended. They were man and wife.

"To make this perfectly legal," said the priest, "we need your name, Sheriff."

"Father Connell," said the sheriff, "I dunno much about these things, but I figure it's all right for me to go into a thing where you're leading the way."

In that way the sheriff became a witness to the marriage of the outlaw on whose trail he was riding.

Afterward the departure came quickly. Horses were led out; the girl and Lucky mounted in the dim starlight.

"Bud," said the big man, "are you coming?"

"I'm stayin' behind," answered Bud, "to fix things so's you and Molly can come back home."

"God bless you, Bud. But you ain't kissed the bride yet."

He stooped; Bud was caught beneath the arms and swept up into the air, and soft lips touched his forehead.

Afterward he was swung gently down to the ground and stood dazed, with his hand to his face, while the two figures melted into the night.

"Gee," said Bud. "I feel like I'd been shot!"

"And now, Father Connell," said the sheriff, "I guess it's your part to explain these things to the men inside the house."

"My part?" exclaimed the priest. "My dear sheriff,

this is certainly your own work! I have been, you might say, compelled to take part in the ceremony. But whoever heard of forcing Sheriff Nevil?''

The sheriff groaned. From the house rolled out the chorus of a new song, led by the mighty voice of Mr. Aiken.

''Gents,'' said Bud, ''foller me. I'll do the talking.''

Max Brand is the best-known pen name of Frederick Faust, creator of Dr. Kildare, Destry, and many other fictional characters popular with readers and viewers worldwide. Faust wrote for a variety of audiences in many genres. His enormous output, totaling approximately thirty million words or the equivalent of 530 ordinary books, covered nearly every field: crime, fantasy, historical romance, espionage, Westerns, science fiction, adventure, animal stories, love, war, and fashionable society, big business and big medicine. Eighty motion pictures have been based on his work along with many radio and television programs. For good measure he also published four volumes of poetry. Perhaps no other author has reached more people in more different ways.

Born in Seattle in 1892, orphaned early, Faust grew up in the rural San Joaquin Valley of California. At Berkeley he became a student rebel and one-man literary movement, contributing prodigiously to all campus publications. Denied a degree because of unconventional conduct, he embarked on a series of adventures culminating in New York City where, after a period of near starvation, he received simultaneous recognition as a serious poet and successful popular-prose writer. Later, he traveled widely, making his home in New York, then in Florence, and finally in Los Angeles.

Once the United States entered the Second World War, Faust abandoned his lucrative writing career and his work as a screenwriter to serve as a war correspondent with the infantry in Italy, despite his fifty-one years and a bad heart. He was killed during a night attack on a hilltop village held by the German army. New books based on magazine serials or unpublished manuscripts continue to appear. Alive and dead he has averaged a new one every four months for seventy-five years. In the U.S. alone nine publishers issue his work, plus many more in foreign countries. Yet, only recently have the full dimensions of this extraordinarily versatile and prolific writer come to be recognized and his stature as a protean literary figure in the 20th Century acknowledged. His popularity continues to grow throughout the world.

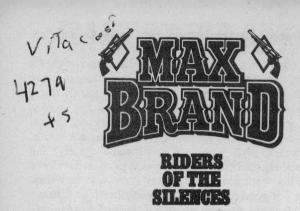

Vitacost
4279
+5

MAX BRAND

RIDERS OF THE SILENCES

"Brand is a topnotcher!"
—New York Times

He sweeps down from the north like a cold blast of death. His name is Red Pierre, and he is bent on drawing blood. The locals say the man he hunts can't be beaten. But six years of riding with a wolf pack have left Red Pierre with a burning hate and a steady trigger finger. Now he is going to get the bushwhacker who shot his father. And if his six-guns can't put the yellowbelly six feet under, he'll go after his gutless enemy with his bare hands.

_3838-2 $4.50 US/$5.50 CAN

TIMBAL GULCH TRAIL

MAX BRAND

"Brand is a topnotcher!"
—*New York Times*

Les Burchard owns the local gambling palace, half the town, and most of the surrounding territory, and Walt Devon's thousand-acre ranch will make him king of the land. The trouble is, Devon doesn't want to sell. In a ruthless bid to claim the spread, Burchard tries everything from poker to murder. But Walt Devon is a betting man by nature, even when the stakes are his life. The way Devon figures, the odds are stacked against him, so he can either die alone or take his enemy to the grave with him.

___3828-5 $4.50 US/$5.50 CAN